Three Tequilas

TRICIA O'MALLEY

Copyright © 2016 by Tricia O'Malley
All Rights Reserved.

Cover Design: Alchemy Book Covers
Editor: Elayne Morgan

All rights reserved. No part of this book may be reproduced in any form by any means without express permission of the author. This includes reprints, excerpts, photocopying, recording, or any future means of reproducing text.

If you would like to do any of the above, please seek permission first by contacting the author at: tricia@thestolendog.com

"Only the Devil and I know the whereabouts of my treasure; and the one of us who lives the longest should take it all." – Edward "Blackbeard" Teach

Chapter One

"I CAN'T BELIEVE I'm being asked to be a part of a research team," I marveled to Luna as she examined her face in front of a cut glass mirror hanging on her side of the Potions & Tarot shop we owned. Like she had anything to worry about. She and I both knew she used magick to keep the threat of wrinkles away from her untainted beautiful skin.

"Althea Rose, there is absolutely no reason you *wouldn't* be asked to be a part of a research team," Luna turned and scoffed, hands on her delicate hips. Everything about Luna was delicate – from her slim build to her graceful cheekbones to the blonde sweep of her hair.

She could even wear white without getting it dirty.

I still hadn't gotten over that particular annoyance with Luna. She was my best friend and business partner, and we were about as alike as roses and dandelions. But our differences did little to keep us apart and the bond between us was stronger for it.

Someday I was going to get her spell for keeping white clothes clean.

Even if I had to hold the scrawny bitch down and sit on her.

Luna narrowed her eyes at me.

"You just got a decidedly evil look on your face. What were you just thinking about?"

I smiled sweetly at her and pushed my mass of dark curls over my shoulder. This month I'd added some caramel streaks to my hair – which was fairly subdued for me. I was trying to tone it down a notch, as my boyfriend, Cash, led a far more normal life than I did.

Being a psychic and all could be a bit off-putting for most people.

And it was the "and all" part that I was still trying to figure out.

"Nothing, I was just thinking about how to get out of my next magick lesson." I smiled brightly at Luna.

"Thea, you know you have magick. We've discovered that you're stronger than you realize. Don't you want to harness that power? You have no problem doing so for your tarot card readings – why can't you do it with spells and rituals?" Luna shook her head at me – her blonde hair swinging like a curtain. "Most people would be ecstatic to know they have the level of power that you do. And here I am dragging you like a recalcitrant toddler to your lessons."

I snorted. I'd only thrown one tantrum, hadn't I?

"I just want to read cards and take underwater photographs. Is that too much to ask?"

"Yes, it is. When you are ignoring your goddess-given gift, it damn well is. I'm not saying you have to start joining me on all my rituals and start mixing up magick tonics. I'm just asking that you continue to learn how to safely practice magick. Goddess forbid you get stuck in another situation and try to run a spell all willy-nilly and what not." Luna shuddered delicately. Did I mention she does *everything* delicately? I probably did.

"I can't imagine that sleepy Tequila Key is going to have too much drama after the last few incidents. I suspect we'll be cruising along just fine for a while here," I said, crossing to examine a box full of crystals on the counter.

Tequila Key was one of the overlooked Keys on the trek down to the tourist hot spot of Key West. Years ago, an over-exuberant mayor had posted a sign off the highway proclaiming *Tequila Makes It Better*, forever sealing our status as an ignored destination. Tourists would hop out of their cars, take a silly picture by the sign, and continue the cruise down to Key West.

The crab shack guy who'd set up next to the sign was making a killing, though.

Tequila Key is divided into two distinct sections – the old section where the likes of me lived, and the new section, recently renamed Port Atticus, which housed whitewashed mansions and manicured lawns. A few years back, the Whittiers, one of Tequila Key's founding families, had begun a campaign to invite wealthy homeowners down to Tequila Key by offering a break on property taxes. It had worked – and I had to admit I didn't mind the tax break.

Even if it meant I had to put up with the Prudie and Theodore Whittiers of the world.

Luna and I ran our Luna Rose Potions & Tarot shop in the older section of Tequila Key. We'd renovated a small clapboard cottage with two front doors to turn it into a divided shop. On Luna's side, everything was white on white on white. With whitewashed floors and some gold accents, her shop was all elegance. In it, she sold handmade soaps, tonics, elixirs, and other healing gifts. Maybe she put a little charm into each as well – but that's why they commanded such a high price. People were willing to pay more when magick was involved.

My side of the shop looked like the room of a rowdy teenager who refused to clean up. There was lots of leopard print, purple velvet, and crowded shelves full of various psychic antiquities and oddities that my mother sent me from her travels around the world. I'm certain that most of them had more magick than I even knew what to do with – but Abigail Rose played her cards close to her chest.

I'd only recently discovered that, aside from my mother being one of the most famous psychics in the world, she also was a sorceress.

Thanks for the heads up, Mom.

Luna was determined to hunt Abigail down and have a major talk with her, but my mother was off in another corner of the world – Myanmar at the moment, I believe. She was on the yacht of someone dangerously wealthy and quietly famous, and I'm sure she and my father were having the time of their lives.

Diving's good there, I hear.

"Stop trying to distract me – what's the deal with the research team?" Luna asked as she began to unpack her box of crystals, holding each one up to the light and examining it carefully before setting it down on the counter.

"A professor from some fancy-schmancy institute in London contacted Trace – if you can believe that. It seems he's discovered an old manuscript, a treasure map of sorts, that leads to an undiscovered shipwreck. It's believed to be from a Spanish treasure fleet. If what he says is true, it's likely that the shipwreck could hold billions of dollars in salvageable treasure," I said, a shiver of excitement and anticipation racing through me.

"And they want you to document it?" Luna asked.

"They want me to document it. Apparently they like Trace's reputation as a dive master, and they researched my website to see if I was capable of the level of underwater photography they're looking for. It seems I am, and they've rented Trace's boat out privately for the next couple weeks, along with a generous stipend for my time."

"Well, shit, add scientific researcher to your resume,"

Luna squealed.

"I feel like I already have enough things on my resume." It was true, too. Between being a full-time psychic and selling underwater pictures across the world, more work was the last thing I needed. But I couldn't hide the fact that I was flattered the big-shots at the research institute were willing to have me catalogue their treasure hunt.

"You're going on a treasure hunt," Luna pointed out, moving across the room with a crystal in her hand. "It's like every kid's dream come true."

"Every adult's, too. Could you imagine the split of the treasure?"

"How does that work? Will you get any part of it?"

"Hard to say. It depends on how far offshore the wreck is. If it's close to land, Florida can claim it. If it isn't, well, it's up in the air. I know Trace said we have some contracts to go over in the morning, which I assume details the fine print. It would be cool to keep a piece or two, though."

"A piece or two?" Luna snorted and put her hands on her hips. "A gold doubloon is not just 'a piece or two' of some silly treasure. That's big bucks you're talking about."

"Well, so? I mean if there is loads of treasure on the ship – what's one little doubloon?"

Chapter Two

It appeared that it *was* big deal, after all.

The gold doubloon, that is.

The next morning I found myself huddled over contracts at Beanz, the local coffee shop. Trace had insisted on meeting me there instead of at the dive boat, which is how I knew he was taking this venture very seriously.

"Nothing? Nothing at *all?*" I squeaked, raising my eyebrows at Trace over the contracts stacked in front of us. We were seated at a small table stuck in the corner of the coffee shop. Regulars bustled in and out, waving a hand to us in greeting, as Trace leaned back and crossed tattooed and well-tanned arms over his chest.

"You can't take any of the treasure," Trace said patiently.

I bit back a sigh. One of these days I was going to have to get a hold on my attraction for Trace. I was in the middle of a relationship with a very hot and decidedly yummy millionaire who had pretty much everything a woman could want. So why was I still looking sideways at my dive buddy?

Trace and I had been friends ever since he'd moved to Tequila Key six or seven years ago. With his easygoing manner, tall lanky frame, and killer blue eyes, women flocked to him on sight. He'd built up a strong reputation for being an excellent dive master, and together we'd explored a lot of unknown spots – him just for the pleasure of diving without leading a crew, and me for working on my underwater photography. Our friendship had been easygoing and platonic through the years, with me often offering counsel on his various love interests. It wasn't until Cash, my current boyfriend, had come to town and lasered in on me that Trace had suddenly made his move.

Shitty timing, right?

Months later, we found ourselves in a standoff of sorts. I continued to date Cash, and Trace was currently dating some slip of a girl who liked to wear thong bikinis. But I'd be lying if I said my view of Trace hadn't shifted just a bit.

"Earth to Althea," Trace said, snapping his fingers under my nose.

"Sorry." I shook my head and focused back on the contracts at hand. "So you're saying a gold doubloon is worth how much?"

"In the current market? Depending on age, condition,

and what boat it comes off of – I'd say close to a million."

"For just *one* of them?" I squeaked, fanning my face dramatically with my hand. Trace laughed, his teeth flashing white in his tanned face.

"Just one of them."

"This is off Treasure Coast, right? The eleven ships that were lost transporting pearls, emeralds, and gold from Cuba to Spain?"

What? I'd been known to listen in on a history class once in a while. And I liked to know the history of wrecks in my area. As a diver, you never know what you might stumble across.

"Yes, though four of the eleven ships have never been found. Stupid commanding officer," Trace snorted.

He was right, too. The commanding officer of the fleet had, senselessly, decided to sail right before hurricane season. In a matter of one week, all eleven ships had been lost, along with the lives of everyone on board. It was one of the greatest tragedies to ever befall a treasure fleet expedition. And there was still treasure to be found. Billions of dollars' worth, or so it seemed from the contracts I was currently reading.

"Though I don't think it's the doubloons they are really after," Trace added as an afterthought.

"What else are they looking for?"

"Well..." Trace ran his hand through his sun-streaked hair and looked around before bending closer and lowering his voice. "I'm fairly certain it may involve a legend of sorts."

"A legend," I breathed. This venture had suddenly taken on a whole new aspect. "From like a saint or something? From where?"

"You know how certain items in history have legends surrounding them? Like the Hope Diamond or the Holy Grail?"

I nodded, gesturing with my iced coffee for him to continue.

"Well, there's an emerald that is mentioned in here – El Serpiente. I did some research,, and, well, if we find it – watch out."

"The Serpent?" I asked, translating the Spanish phrase.

"Yes, green stone named for the green-eyed serpent. From what I can remember of my shoddy history class, when the Spanish invaded Mexico to gather treasure, somehow the history or legends get intermixed on Quetzalcoatl – the Aztec feather serpent god."

"Sure, I've heard of him."

"I'm not entirely sure if he's strictly a Mexican or an Aztec god, but the legends of this god were taken back to Spain by explorers. Along with an emerald. The size of my fist." Trace held up his fist, tightly closed. "The emerald is said to have been handed down as the stone of Quetzalcoatl, who is considered the God of the Morning Star – of light, truth, and justice. It's believed that whoever possesses the stone becomes almost god-like himself – that it imbues the wearer with great powers."

"No," I breathed.

"People have been searching for El Serpiente for hundreds of years. The stone, once held by Cortes himself, was supposedly lost along with many other Aztec treasures and relics."

"But it wasn't?"

Trace shook his head.

"This professor seems to think the stone ended up on one of the boats that was heading from Cuba to Spain in 1715 before the storms sunk them."

I let that sit with me for a moment.

"So what you're saying is that a legendary emerald, presumably with god-like powers, has been tracked to a wreck off the coast of Florida?"

Trace nodded sagely.

"Holy shit," I breathed, taking a sip of my iced coffee as I absorbed this news. "Is it like the Holy Grail? People can live forever?"

Trace shrugged one shoulder, his lips pressed in a tight line.

"I don't really know. All I know is that I had to sign a confidentiality agreement to even read through this contract, and that it is some major shit. And I shouldn't even be talking to you about it without your signature on a confidentiality agreement."

I shivered as his words went through me. This was big deal stuff right here – leaders of nations had sought this emerald for centuries. And we might be the ones to find it.

"Oh, I'm *so* in," I gushed.

I mean, what could go wrong?

Famous last words. I rolled my eyes at myself. I should know better than to think something like that. And thinking it was just as bad as saying it out loud, as far as I'm concerned.

"Well, sign the confidentiality agreement first. Then we'll dig deeper," Trace said, looking over his shoulder as he slid the paper at me. I scanned the single page document – a fairly boilerplate non-disclosure agreement – and signed it quickly before pushing the paper back at him.

"Talk."

"Okay, so this professor? Professor Johansson? Well, I think he has a pretty major backer on this project. He referred to it only as a 'private investor' and stressed that money was no object. I can't even imagine how much El Serpiente would fetch at auction, but I'm sure it'd be a pretty penny."

I tapped my finger against my lips as I thought about it.

"I know there's that famous emerald up at the Smithsonian or something. Let me Google it." I pulled out my iPhone and typed it in. "Gachala Emerald, 858 carats. Wow, it doesn't even list the value. That's a huge stone," I murmured, scrolling through more information.

"Here's another tidbit – the Spanish royal family liked to wear emeralds to add some much-needed color to the dark clothes they wore. The Nuestra Senora de Atocha," I nodded in recognition of the name of a famous shipwreck off the coast of the Keys, "which sunk in 1622, was carrying over six thousand emeralds destined for the Spanish royal family. The emeralds discovered from the ship have been valued at over $400 million."

I raised an eyebrow at Trace.

"Yowza."

"I'll say. So, we know that Spain's royal family liked emeralds, and there's a famous one rumored to carry mythological powers of an Aztec god. Professor Johansson from London, who is being bankrolled by an anonymous investor, believes he's located the famous emerald, plus whatever other treasures this shipwreck may hold. Am I summing that up correctly?"

Trace took a bite of his bagel and leaned back, crossing his arms over his chest.

"Sounds about right."

"Okay. Let's muddle through these contracts. I don't like to sign anything unless my lawyer goes over it too."

"I already had my lawyer go through them. Nothing dodgy, just that they are very specific about the confidentiality of the expedition, that all images are owned by them – not us – and that all information on the whereabouts of the wreck is exclusive information to them."

"Basically we saw nothing, we heard nothing, and we know nothing," I grumbled as I swirled my spoon around in my yogurt parfait. My psychic senses were telling me this was going to be big trouble.

And yet the little girl deep inside of me screamed that she wanted to go on a treasure hunt.

"Hard to turn down an honest-to-god treasure hunt, isn't it?" I mused, pointing a finger at Trace.

His smile flashed across his face again.

"I knew you wouldn't be able to resist."

"May the goddess help us all," I said to Trace as I held my hand across the table to shake his, ignoring the tingles that went through me when his hand touched my palm. "When do I meet this professor?"

"Tomorrow morning. We'll pick him up from his hotel. Be ready," Trace sent me a cheeky wink. "We ride at dawn."

CHAPTER THREE

EVEN THOUGH I knew the potential for danger was high, I couldn't help but be excited about the expedition. I wondered what El Serpiente looked like – was it set in gold? Cut or uncut? I daydreamed about a mythological serpent god dancing around a fire, wearing the emerald around his neck.

Quetzalcoatl.

The stuff of legends, really.

I pedaled my bike lazily away from downtown Tequila Key, turning down a lane to cruise by Miss Elva's house to see if she was out front. Miss Elva, Tequila Key's resident voodoo priestess, had an attitude larger than life – and the wardrobe to match.

I also considered her one of my best friends.

"Here comes trouble. Awful early for you to be out and about on a Sunday, ain't it? Shouldn't you be at church? Or wound around that handsome hunk of eye candy you've hooked?" Miss Elva slapped her knee as she hollered to me from where she sat on the front porch of her two-story shingle home. She'd placed a comfy rocking chair with bright cushions in her favorite corner of the porch, and often spent time watching the world go by.

She didn't welcome visitors all that often, if the hard, straight-backed, single wooden chair – with no cushions, mind you – was any indication. But I knew my presence was always welcome.

For the most part.

"Church? Aren't you the funny one! I'm communing with nature on this beautiful morning that the Goddess has bestowed upon us." I grinned up at Miss Elva as I perched my bike against the railing of her porch steps and climbed up to see her. I eyed the visitor's chair and decided to stand instead. Leaning back against the railing, I crossed my arms over my chest and took in today's outfit.

Miss Elva smiled up at me, a brilliant orange caftan, with peacock feathers around the wrists and lining the hem, covering her generous body. A matching peacock feather was tucked in her hair amidst the intricate braids woven around her head and up to a bun at the top. She looked every inch the regal queen, and a part of me wished I could be Miss Elva when I grew up.

"Looking smashing as always," I said.

Miss Elva drew a critical eye over my outfit.

"I can't say the same for you, child. What did you do –

roll right out of bed and go for a bike ride?"

"Hey! It's not that bad," I said, smoothing a hand down my rumpled black maxi dress.

"Child, please. I know what I'm looking at, don't I? Now, what's got you up and about this morning? Why aren't you with Cash?"

"Cash left early this morning to go up to Miami to sign a contract. He should be back tomorrow afternoon and then staying for a whole week this time – it'll be nice to have him around."

"He still looking at property down here?"

I shrugged. He'd mentioned it a while ago – but the conversation about him moving here had stalled out recently.

"We'll see."

Miss Elva harrumphed and rocked once in her chair before looking back at me.

"You just out for coffee then?"

"Actually, I met with Trace. We've got a…" I thought about it for a moment. I'd signed a confidentiality agreement so I had to be careful what I said. But Miss Elva was old magick – so if I told her to read my mind, it wasn't technically breaking the contract.

"What am I thinking of?" I asked Miss Elva in lieu of answering her question. I focused on the emerald and its name, hoping she would pluck it from my head.

Miss Elva's pretty brown eyes narrowed as she studied me for a moment. Then her eyebrows rose and she let out a low whistle.

"Tell me you aren't trying to find El Serpiente."

"Bingo." I breathed out a sigh of relief, happy that I had stayed within the terms of my contract. There was a lot of money on the table, and I could see a vacation to Europe or someplace lovely hovering on the horizon once I got paid. For the most part, I made more than enough money to live on: My townhouse was paid off, I had no car payment, and I had a cushy savings in the bank. Don't let the stereotypes of psychics fool you - the tarot world can be a very lucrative business. It didn't hurt that Luna was excellent with money and kept an eagle eye on my finances as well as her own.

But still – it wasn't every day you were offered a $50,000 paycheck for a few weeks of work.

"Fifty thousand dollars! Whooo, honey. What have you gone and gotten yourself into now?" Miss Elva tilted her head at me and began to rock her chair in earnest – a sure sign she was becoming agitated.

I sighed. Who was I kidding? I was totally going to tell Miss Elva all the details. With my luck, she'd probably be the one who'd save me or find El Serpiente. It was never a bad thing to have Miss Elva in my back pocket.

"It's a research team from London, led by one Professor Johansson. It's all very hush-hush. Trace will help them find their coordinates and lead the dives, and I'll be taking pictures and documenting everything. They were clear that they own all the rights to the treasure, as well as the copyright to all the pictures."

"What do you know about that stone?"

"Just what Trace told me over coffee this morning. I've come right from there with no time to research it more."

"That there stone does not need to be falling into the wrong hands. Powerful stuff you're messing in, Miss Thing." Miss Elva's rocking picked up pace.

"I mean, is it really an Aztec god's stone?" I wasn't about to try and pronounce the name that Trace had managed to pronounce at breakfast.

"So the legend goes. The feathered serpent. He always wore a particular talisman, and the stone was rumored to be an emerald as big as an ostrich egg. Many spells and great powers were said to be infused into that stone. It's not a thing to be trifled with. It can take over, you know."

I raised an eyebrow at her, then turned to scan the street when I heard a car door slam. I held my hand up to wave to the neighbor, then turned back to Miss Elva.

"Take over how? Explain, please."

"You know, stones are meant for their masters. That type of stone at least. If it can sense it's more powerful than you, it can take over. For example, if it falls into the wrong hands, it may feed off the strongest emotion of the person holding it. Say the person is really greedy, which I'm assuming they would be if they're trying to get their hands on El Serpiente – well, the stone can feed off that and compel the person to do far more harm than their original intentions. It takes a powerful hand to rule a powerful stone. You must remember that while they are tools and talismans, they do have their own energy. Some are conduits for energy, and some give off energy. El Serpiente is both."

I dug my toe into a floorboard of her porch.

"This is bad, then?"

"I suggest that if you find it, *you* be the one to recover it. And before you do so, get some training from Luna on how to hold a stone in a stasis state. She'll teach you the spell. You'll need it, most likely."

"I highly doubt the research team will let me hold the stone."

"And I'm telling you that it's your *job* to get your hands on it before they do. This *is* bad. Some things are meant to remain uncovered, and this is one of them. It's meant to stay buried."

"Here I thought this was going to be some miraculous recovery – maybe something that could be added to a museum. And now you're making it sound like it's going to take over the world."

"Child, when that stone was stolen and on its trip back to Spain, eleven ships sank and hundreds of men died in a matter of days. *Days*. Think about that. What would possess a seafaring man, who's studied the weather and commanded ships all his grown life, to set sail right before hurricane season? He was blinded by the riches, blinded by power, and blinded by the stone. El Serpiente wanted him to sail – just like it wanted them all to die. The stone never should have been taken from that temple. You know that's what happened, don't you? It was stolen from an Aztec temple. And it cost the Spanish fleet their lives."

Her words made goosebumps rise on my arms, even though the mid-morning heat was already close to eighty degrees. Sure, the stuff of legends gets added to and embossed over the years – but this was Miss Elva, and she always gave it to you straight.

"You think I should back out."

It wasn't really a question, but I had to know.

"I think that if it's going to be found, better for it to be by someone like you, who's more comfortable with magickal things and can diffuse some of its power for a while. At least until you can get it to Luna and me, where we can work our magick on it."

"What makes you think they'll let me get that far with the stone?"

Miss Elva leveled her gaze at me. "You'll have to make it happen."

"Great. Real stinking great."

"You signed the contract, honeychild, not me. But you know I'll help you."

I blew out a breath and nodded my thanks.

"Tell Rafe I said hi, by the way. Wherever he is."

Rafe was Miss Elva's pirate ghost and a regular fixture by her side. He was deeply in love with Miss Elva, loved to tell tales of his seafaring days, and was an all-around lecherous old coot. But we all loved him.

Well, those of us who could see and hear him, that is.

"Child, he's sleeping in this morning," Miss Elva scoffed and shook her head, looking up at me. "Like a damn ghost needs any sleep."

Chapter Four

A SWIPE OF tongue across my face jolted me from a dream of being on a ship at sea, riding out a storm.

"Hank!" I gasped, holding a hand to my heart. I shifted to look at my Boston terrier, Hank, as he looked at me quizzically from his spot on the pillow next to me. Taking a deep breath, I tried to calm myself down. The dream had seemed so real – I could almost taste the spray of salt water on my lips.

Slanting a look at the clock, I groaned. Don't you just hate it when you wake up twenty minutes before your alarm? Not like I'd gotten much sleep to speak of. I'd spent much of my Sunday sitting on the porch with my laptop, throwing a ball for Hank and researching El Serpiente.

What I'd found had confirmed Miss Elva's information – and added to it. From what I could piece together, the Spanish Treasure Fleet hadn't been the first expedition to steal El Serpiente. There had been several attempts made prior to that.

And each expedition had ended in death.

I cuddled Hank closer as I gulped at the thought. Statistically speaking, 100% of the people who had sought to claim El Serpiente had died.

Odds were not in my favor on this one.

I sighed and kissed Hank's head. "I hope I didn't get myself in over my head this time," I told him. He reached out and pawed my hand – his sign that he wanted me to scratch his belly.

Oh well – I was in it now. I'd signed the contracts.

Though as far as I was concerned, contracts could be broken. I was going to take this one moment at a time – and if my spidey senses signaled danger, then I was out. I'd had more than enough brushes with death in recent months. I was determined to live a more normal life.

But who am I kidding? I'm a psychic with apparent magickal powers.

Hank squirmed against me, annoyed that I had stopped scratching his tummy.

"Listen bud, today's an early one. But I've got Miss Elva stopping by at lunch to play with you. You love Miss Elva and she spoils you like all get-out. So don't get mad that we're getting up earlier than usual." I sighed as I pushed myself from the bed. Just shy of five A.M. was not among my normal waking hours, but Trace had wanted us to get an early start so we'd be ready to hit the water just as the sun came up. It was typically the best time to dive anyway – visibility was better and the water might be calmer.

Hank tilted his head at me in question as I slid from the bed and stretched, grumbling through my morning routine, then stepped in front of my closet to grab a cover-up and swim suit.

"Let's go," I said, and Hank launched himself from the bed, his nails clattering across the floor as he raced downstairs to wait by the back door.

The dream stayed with me as I slid the back door open for Hank to go do his business, shuffled through making coffee, and poured some granola in a bowl. I was familiar with life on the water, as I dove weekly and was on a boat pretty much every other day. People in Tequila Key made their living from various water sports, fishing, and other tours. We all lived and breathed the ocean.

It wasn't like we weren't familiar with the dangers of the ocean. In fact, because we lived in harmony with it, we all had nothing but respect for the water. But that didn't negate the very real fear I'd felt in my dream as I'd grasped a rope in my hands and held tight while another swell of water had crossed the bow of the ship. It had been a nasty, take-no-prisoners type of storm, and I shivered again as I relived the sight of men getting swept overboard, right before the crack of the mast breaking in half had cut through the storm and I'd met the captain's eyes in horror.

I would do well to remember the fear – and stay on

edge – as I moved forward with this expedition, I thought. Though we were a long way out from hurricane season, there were other dangers that walked in this world.

Like humans and their greed.

I finished packing my dive gear and called to Hank. He danced around my feet as I opened his toy drawer. Yes, he has a toy drawer. I'd figured out long ago that rotating his toys out kept them fresh and exciting to him.

"Ohhh, your snake!" I squealed, holding up a long green and yellow snake with a row of squeakers tucked inside. Hank whipped around in a circle, his little body quivering with excitement. I smiled as I launched the toy across the room and he skidded after it.

The sound of delighted squeaking met me as I closed and locked my front door.

Then I paused as I realized the little sign the Universe had just given me.

The snake.

"Cute, real cute."

Chapter Five

"Iced coffee with white mocha for the lady," Trace intoned from the front seat of his old Jeep, parked at the curb in front of my townhouse.

I lived at the end of a dead-end street where a row of townhouses squashed together, all painted different bright colors. I loved my little secret slice of paradise —my backyard opened up to a small hidden beach. I'm telling you – if you can find waterfront property in the Keys you can afford, snatch it up. I'd had a construction crew come in to add some sand and level out some of the more rocky areas, and Hank and I were able to wade into the water and play. It was a perfect spot for me and I couldn't be happier that I'd found it.

"Just what I needed. I've only had one hit of coffee so far this morning," I said, swinging my dive gear into the back of Jeep before coming around to slide into the passenger seat.

"I know what you like," Trace said, deliberately looking up at me from under heavy eyelids, a smirk on his face. It was his patented flirting look and I'd see more than one girl – far weaker than I, of course – fall for it.

"Well, thank goodness someone does," I breathed back, pushing my cleavage together and batting my eyes at him.

Trace barked out a laugh and pulled the Jeep from the curb.

"Fighting fire with fire, I see," he smiled over at me, our friendly balance restored.

"I'm a fighter, as you know," I pointed out, taking a sip of the delicious concoction.

"Which is why you're perfect for this expedition," Trace said.

"Well, I certainly hope I won't have to fight anyone or anything," I said, turning to look at him. His eyes were highlighted in the glow from the dashboard, the early dawn at its darkest.

"I'm sure it'll be fine," Trace said, but his tone sounded forced.

"Trace, did you research this? Not one expedition that has tried to take El Serpiente has survived. I don't like it."

There, I'd voiced my fears.

"Well, luckily we've got a lot more technology on our side now. I don't think there's been an expedition on this particular ship since it was lost. A lot has changed in three hundred years. We have sonar, radar, cell phones, solid diving gear, and a good boat. I'm confident things will be different this time."

I held onto those words as we drew closer to the hotel.

Perched on one side of Tequila Key, the Tarpon Inn was a cute motel where the rooms were arranged in a small strip set off from the main office. Painted a violent turquoise shade with hot pink doors, it wasn't the type of place where I'd have thought an esteemed professor would choose to stay. Not that we had a lot of options in Tequila Key – but I'd certainly expected him to be staying somewhere like the sleek Seashore Sands Hotel in the fancy part of town.

"The Tarpon Inn, huh? Not exactly what I was expecting," I said to Trace, as he pulled into a parking spot in the near-empty parking lot. One lone light shone in the front office, but I knew it was for show. Nancy, who ran the inn, would be upstairs sleeping. The front office didn't open until 8:00 am.

"I know, I said the same. But Professor Johansson insisted he wasn't fussy. It seems he was given a stipend for traveling – and the less he spends on hotel costs, the more ends up in his pocket."

"I suppose that's economical of him," I shrugged. "Though wouldn't you think he'd want something with a little more security? What with this being such a high-stakes mission and all?"

Trace laughed at me, the sound long and low, sending a tingle through my belly. I ignored the tingle, but smiled back at him.

"I don't know if I would call this a 'high-stakes mission.' It's not like we're on a covert op or something like that. We're just helping these guys with some research."

"Right. 'Research' that'll yield them millions of dollars and the find of the decade. But, you know, not high stakes at all." I slurped my coffee and eyed the motel.

"I mean, it's probably super exciting for a bunch of stuffy administrators holed up in their offices. But it's just business as usual for us, right? It's not like we get a piece of the pie or anything," Trace pointed out, drumming his hands on the wheel.

"Which is kind of stupid, actually, now that I think about it. Why go on an expedition that has, historically, always yielded bad results without getting anything for it?" I scoffed and leaned forward, taking a hair-tie off my wrist and twisting my curls into a bun on top of my head.

"Oh? Since when is fifty thousand dollars nothing?" Trace slanted a look at me.

"Okay, fine, you've got a point," I grumbled.

"Don't act like you aren't super excited about going on a treasure hunt as well as getting a huge chunk of change in your bank account," I said.

His smile flashed in the light coming from the front of the motel.

"Oh, I'm excited. I feel like a little kid on Christmas

morning."

"Well, it's time to get started. Is he supposed to meet us at the car? Do we go knock?" I said, my eyes on the hotel. None of the lights were on in any of the rooms. As I began to really focus on the motel, instead of on the conversation with Trace, my psychic instincts kicked in.

"Trace…" I interrupted a spiel he was giving about the rudeness of people who are always late.

"What?"

"I've got a really bad feeling about this," I said softly, my eyes trained on the motel.

Trace was well aware of my psychic abilities, so he didn't discount what I was saying or waste time arguing. Instead, he reached into the console and pulled out a small handgun while handing me a diver's knife. My mouth dropped open in shock.

"You own a gun?"

"Yes. Unfortunately, I've found that hanging out with you often requires being armed."

"What! As if!" I exclaimed.

Trace raised an eyebrow at me.

"Maybe only once or twice," I mumbled, unsheathing the knife. "Whatever. Now's not the time. Do you know what room he's in?"

"Room six."

"Let's go check it out."

"Maybe you should let me. Do you think we need to call the police?"

I thought about it.

"I'm going to say yes. But there's no way I'm going to just sit around waiting until the police get here."

"I figured as much. We might as well go knock on his door," Trace said, slipping his cell phone into his back pocket, the gun held comfortably in his hand. The sight of Trace with a gun in his hand made my stomach turn – and not in a good way. I'm not a big fan of guns, and hate the finality they represent.

"Stay behind me," Trace whispered as we walked quietly towards the professor's room.

"Uh-huh," I said, ignoring Trace and walking next to him, already lost in my head as I reached out to scan the room for a mental signature.

"Shit," Trace swore, at the same time I exclaimed, "This is bad."

"No shit, Sherlock," Trace swore again and pointed at the bottom of the door, where a small puddle of blood had leaked beneath the doorframe. It gleamed dully in the low light, as out of place on the doorstep as the gun was in Trace's hand.

This shouldn't be happening, I thought.

Trace kicked in the door and I jumped back, surprised at his ninja-like moves.

"Shit, shit, shit," Trace said, immediately turning to shield me from the view.

It was too late, though. I'd already seeing the professor's glassy eyes staring at the wall, a mass of blood staining the tiles below him.

Chapter Six

EVEN THOUGH THE morning was warm, I'd wrapped a sarong around my shoulders to ward off the chill that seeing death up close had brought on me. I sat on the stoop in front of the motel, dully registering the police activity that swarmed around me.

"Tea," Trace said, nudging my shoulder as he sat next to me and handed me a paper cup.

"Thanks," I said softly.

"I figured you were coffeed out."

"I am. I'm jittery as all hell," I admitted, leaning into him, just a little, for support. Trace took the cue and wrapped his arm around my shoulder, pulling me close.

"I'm sorry you had to see that," Trace said.

"Yeah, 'cause it's your fault? Please. I'm a big girl. I just… it doesn't get easier, is all. I've seen a couple of dead bodies now – well, people who met an unfortunate end –

and it doesn't get any easier. I honestly don't know how cops do it. Seeing death all the time like that? No thank you." I sighed and took a sip of tea. "It's just... it's so incredibly sad, you know? It's not right. Life shouldn't be ended that way."

Even though I knew that death wasn't really the end – after all, I do speak to ghosts – it still saddened me.

A throat cleared next to us and I turned, shielding my eyes against the light of the early morning sun as I looked up at Tequila Key's Chief of Police.

"Althea, thanks for staying," Chief Thomas said, his eyes sharp as he measured me. "I have to say – we seem to be finding ourselves in this position more often than I'd like."

"You and me both," I said.

I'd first met Chief Thomas when Trace and I had recovered a dead body on a dive. He'd been working with the Coast Guard at the time, and had since taken over the Chief of Police's job in Tequila Key. This would be the third time we'd met under such circumstances, and I could only imagine what his opinion of me was.

"Can you tell us how he died?" Trace asked.

"It appears to be from the bullet hole in the back of his head – though the coroner will, of course, look for any other causes of death."

"Nobody heard anything?"

"I haven't gotten that far yet. We're just keeping the scene secure for now, and gathering evidence. I'll have to take your formal statements – but for now, can you tell me what you guys were doing here at such an early hour?"

I glanced at Trace and he nodded. Sliding his hand through his hair, he tied it at the back of his neck as he looked up at the Chief.

"We were here to pick him up for a dive. He'd booked the week with us."

Well, it wasn't a lie.

"It's pretty early for a dive, isn't it? And don't they usually meet you at the boat?"

"He's British. Wasn't interested in trying to drive on the other side of the road," Trace pointed out.

"Ah. Can you tell me more about him?"

Trace rattled off his name and occupation, and then shut up. I held my breath for a moment and waited.

"Althea? Do you have anything to add?"

"Nope, I was just along for the ride. I do underwater photography on the side, you know… so I was just coming along to get some more pictures for the blog."

Okay, now I was the liar. But since Trace hadn't offered any information as to why we were taking the professor diving, I wasn't about to either.

"There was an… unusual marking on the wall. It almost looks like a snake. Would you know anything about that?"

I widened my eyes in shock and shook my head at the Chief.

"Can we see it?"

"Will you keep it quiet? Because if it gets out, it could compromise the case," Chief Thomas pointed out.

Shit. Now I felt bad. If he was going to show us something we technically shouldn't be seeing, it wasn't totally fair that we weren't letting him in on our knowledge. I slid a quick glance at Trace and saw a grimace cross his face.

"Yes, we will," Trace said and then cleared his throat. "Um, well."

"Yes?" Chief Thomas waited.

"I think he mentioned something called El Serpiente – which I'm thinking means the serpent," Trace offered.

Chief Thomas jotted it down on his notepad and nodded.

"And that's what he was here for? To find El Serpiente?"

"Maybe. He'd mentioned it a possible interest. But we didn't get too far into it," Trace shrugged and I felt guilty for holding information back from Chief Thomas. He'd come to my rescue on more than one occasion, and hadn't asked too many questions in the process.

"Trace," I said, sliding him a glance.

"Althea," he shot back, and the Chief waited.

"Here's the deal," I said, making up my mind. I pointed to where other officers were working on the crime scene. "That – over there – that's bad news. And if people are killing for it, it's even worse. I'd rather you didn't know any more than we've given you. It's for your own protection. Plus, I don't know who might be around here –

watching us. I'd prefer to make it seem like we're completely ignorant," I said, shrugging with my hands up and shaking my head in the universal "I know nothing" gesture.

I'll say this much, Chief Thomas was quick. He nodded down at us and closed his notebook.

"Thanks, guys. Too bad you weren't able to offer any help," he said loudly, and then gestured for us to follow him. "I'd still like you to take a look at the crime scene to see if anything jumps out at you."

"Sure," I said and Trace stood up, pulling me with him, tucked at his side.

"Are you sure that was a good idea?" Trace murmured into my ear.

I looked up at him and shrugged. "He's always been fair to me."

"You're right. But we need to be careful how far we pull him into this," Trace whispered and I shivered, realizing that we, most certainly, were now in deep.

"Shit, Cash is going to be pissed," I swore.

"What? Pretty boy can't handle this stuff?" Trace asked, delighted to have a reason to take a stab at Cash.

"More like he doesn't want his girlfriend putting herself in danger. And don't even start – it's not like your little hussy wouldn't have screamed and fainted at the sight of blood."

"Children? If you could?" Chief Thomas asked, raising an eyebrow at us.

"Sorry," I said under my breath, and directed my attention to the Chief.

"I'm just going to let you see the drawing on the wall. I don't want you touching anything, and you aren't allowed to step inside the room. Stand right here," Chief Thomas instructed, pointing to a spot in front of the door, just inches from where the blood puddled.

I gulped at the sight of the blood and folded my arms over my chest. Trace kept his arm around my shoulders, and we turned to look into the room.

Thankfully, Professor Johansson's body was covered now, so I was spared having to look at his dead body again. I wondered if they'd closed his eyes. Shaking my head, I looked to where Chief Thomas pointed.

The room – its bright colors screaming *Florida Keys* – was ruined by the damage wreaked upon it. Every drawer in the credenza that lined one bright yellow wall was thrown on the floor, the clothes strewn around the room, and the bedspread was torn from the bed. Noticeably absent were any signs of papers or a computer. Wouldn't a professor bring a computer with him on a research expedition? Before I could ask the question, my eyes landed on the wall that Chief Thomas pointed to.

This wall was painted the same light blue of the tiles, as an accent to the sunny yellow that covered the other three walls of the room. Centered above the bed was an S-shaped design – decidedly crude, yet at the same time surprisingly intricate. It was as though someone had dipped a paintbrush in the Professor's blood; the lines were much thicker than a fingers-width. As I looked at it, it dawned on me that the drawing wasn't deliberately crude. It was a replica.

"I… I think I know what that is," I said, and Chief Thomas' head whipped around to look at me.

"And? I mean, it looks like a snake."

"It's a replica. It's the Aztec depiction of a snake. I've seen it somewhere…in my studies and all," I finished lamely.

"The Aztec depiction of a snake?"

"Yeah. See how the lines form those little triangles and zigzags? It's not meant to be messy. At least that's not the vibe I'm getting."

Trace's arms tightened around my shoulders at my words.

I knew what he was thinking.

El Serpiente's legend was at work.

CHAPTER SEVEN

AFTER PROMISING TO come down to the station later to give our statements, Trace and I left the crime scene, unsure of what to do next.

"I think we need to go to Lucky's. I know the Chief said not to say anything, but I'm starving and I need to call Miss Elva."

"You're thinking rally the troops?" Trace asked.

"I'm thinking we're going to need backup. You know our friends won't say anything. But this is big-evil kind of bad. The likes of which we shouldn't face alone."

"Do you think anything more will come of it? I mean – technically we're off the hook, right? We don't have to dive any more, since the professor is dead."

"Was the contract we signed just with the professor?"

"Ah... no, actually. It was with a subsidiary – I think of the institute. I'm going to have to check that," Trace said as he drove his Jeep towards Lucky's while I texted Miss Elva and Luna to meet us there.

"I can't remember either. I kind of flew through the papers."

"I feel like we'll need to notify the institute too," Trace said, pulling into a spot by Lucky's Tiki Bar.

Lucky's was owned by one of my best friends in the world, Beau. He'd purchased it shortly after high school after receiving an inheritance, and had turned it into the hottest spot for a margarita and cheeseburger in Tequila Key. Perched higher up on a bit of a cliff at the end of the main drag, Lucky's looked like a tiki hut, with a thatched roof, screens to keep out the bugs, and pufferfish lamps hanging from the ceiling. Beau was close to opening his second restaurant at the other end of the strip – one that would bring high-end seafood and steak dinners to downtown. He was smart to cover both ends of the dining spectrum, and I couldn't be more proud of him.

"Think he's open? It's only ten," Trace asked.

"Yeah, he's always here early on Mondays to take inventory," I said, walking up the gravel path and swinging the door open. A long circular teakwood bar dominated the room, and the walls were covered with my underwater photos and fishnets arranged in a kitschy, yet fun, manner. Beau popped his head up from where he was kneeling behind the bar.

"Whooee! Aren't you a sight for sore eyes? I haven't seen you in damn near a week, girl," Beau exclaimed, bringing a hand to his hip and raising an eyebrow at me.

It was mannerisms like this one that gave Beau away as being gay – but to the casual observer, he was just a handsome man, tanned, with a perfect build and a preppy yet surfer-casual cool. I'd watched more than one girl sigh after him as he served drinks in the bar.

I offered Beau a shrug, realizing suddenly that I was dangerously close to tears. He must have seen it too, because he slid out from around the bar, his arms outstretched.

"Come to papa, sweetie. What happened? Did you and Cash have a fight?"

Beau embraced me and I leaned into his solidness, holding on for a moment as he clucked over me. I barely held the tears back, but managed to do so even though there was a lump the size of Texas in my throat.

"We found the client we were supposed to take diving today murdered on the floor of his room at Tarpon Inn," Trace said succinctly.

Beau didn't say a word. Instead he released me and, keeping my hand in his, tugged me over to the bar.

"Sit," he ordered, all but pushing me onto one of the stools.

I sat.

Beau ducked behind the bar and pulled out a bottle of Irish whiskey. Leaning over, he poured out three shots and slid two across the bar for Trace and me.

"Drink."

We drank.

The whiskey burned its way down my throat, breaking through the lump that was lodged there, and screamed its way down to my belly. I met Beau's eyes. He raised the bottle in question.

"One more," I said.

Nodding, Beau poured us another round and we all drank silently. I traced my hand over the smooth wood of the bar, uncertain where to start.

"This had better be good," called Luna's voice from the doorway, and I turned.

As soon as she saw my face, Luna crossed the room and wrapped her arms around me.

"Was it Cash? Did you have a fight?"

I caught Trace's delighted smile.

"Listen, it's natural to think someone is upset about their boyfriend," I hissed at him, and he held up his hands.

"I didn't say anything."

"I know what you were thinking."

"I wasn't thinking anything."

"Yes, you were. Do I look like an idiot?"

"Children, children," Beau said, interrupting us. "Why don't I get some food on? I'm assuming you haven't eaten yet today. Lord knows that whiskey is going to go straight to your head with no food in your stomach."

"That's fine. Miss Elva's on her way too."

"Don't say anything until I'm back. I'll be quick. Promise." Beau was already disappearing into the kitchen.

"Honey, I closed the shop and everything. What's up?" Luna asked, taking a stool next to me. She looked coolly elegant in a light blue linen sheath dress – unwrinkled, of course. It was positively unnatural. Linen was meant to wrinkle, I thought.

I swear – pour a few shots in me on an empty stomach and I turn positively bitchy.

I smiled gratefully as Beau returned from the kitchen long enough to slide a basket of chips and salsa at me.

"Eat," he ordered.

I grabbed a chip and crunched down on it, the salty taste distracting me for a moment.

"Althea?" Luna asked.

"Our dive client was murdered. We found the body," Trace said, snagging a chip.

"Yup. What he said," I mumbled over a mouthful of chips. Once I'd started eating, I wasn't able to stop, and I kept cramming chips in my mouth.

"Whoa, honey, slow down," Luna said gently, putting her hand on my arm.

"It was horrible," I said softly, meeting her eyes.

"What happened?"

"No talking until I'm done in the kitchen," Beau said, poking his head out of the door and yelling at us.

"That's fine. Miss Elva's on the way anyway," I said, grabbing another chip.

"Fine, I'll wait," Luna said, studying the basket until she found the chip she was looking for. She picked it up and began nibbling delicately on a corner of it. I rolled my eyes.

"What?"

"Please, who eats chips like that?"

"I do," Luna smiled at me, clearly happy to see that some of my spunk was coming back.

"Don't get me started on the linen." I pointed at her dress.

"What's wrong with linen? It's perfect for this climate."

I was saved from answering when a delighted bark met my ears.

"Hank!" I exclaimed, jumping up from the stool and crouching down on the floor to meet my delighted dog. He raced across the room and jumped on me, licking my face as he dissolved in wiggles of excitement.

"Something told me he was needed here," Miss Elva said, trailing behind him in a caftan of deep ocean blue shot with threads of purple. Her hair was wrapped in a floral scarf with blue, red, and yellow accents and she breezed into the restaurant without a care in the world.

"Good call," I said, snuggling my face against Hank's chest. I didn't care that I was sitting on the floor of the bar. I was still in my swimsuit and cover up anyway.

"Did I hear Hank?" Beau called from the kitchen.

"You most certainly did, sweetie pie," Miss Elva called.

"I'll throw a mini burger on for him."

THREE TEQUILAS

I swear Hank's ears perked up at the word burger.

"Can we move to a table so Hank can sit on a lower chair?" I asked.

"Sounds good. I'll grab us some drinks," Luna said, moving behind the bar and pulling out a pitcher of iced tea. We both had grown up with Beau and were as at home in his bar as if it were our own.

Just as we settled ourselves at a long table by the windows overlooking the water, Beau swung out of the kitchen with a tray full of food.

"It's all appetizers except for Hank's burger – I wanted to be quick," Beau apologized as he set the tray on the table and distributed baskets of food. Hank sat, alert in his chair, his eyes following every basket that was delivered.

"Don't think I forgot you, Hank buddy," Beau said, sliding a basket in front of Hank. A small burger, no larger than a half dollar, and five French fries were presented as though he were a king. I laughed as Hank vibrated in his seat, looking to me for permission and then back at the basket of food.

"Go ahead," I told Hank, and he jumped in delight, placing his paws on the edge of the table and diving nose-first into the basket. His little body wiggled in pleasure – like all his Christmases had come at once.

"Eat," Beau instructed, pointing to the basket of mozzarella sticks in front of me. He knew me well. Melted cheese was the way to my heart.

The table fell silent as we dug into our food, and I began to feel marginally better as my stomach filled.

"Well, child, go ahead. Who died?" Miss Elva asked breezily, waving a French fry in the air. Hank followed its every move carefully.

"You're kidding, but someone really did," I said to Miss Elva, and she shook her head at me.

"I wasn't kidding. But I want to hear the story."

I gestured to Trace. "Go ahead."

I continued to eat as Trace filled everyone in on our morning. Sneaking Hank a French fry, I ran my hand down his back, happy that Miss Elva had decided to bring him along.

"Did I not tell you El Serpiente was bad news?" Miss Elva asked.

Luna leveled a look at me.

"You told Miss Elva about this and not me?"

"It wasn't like that… I saw her on the way home yesterday is all," I said sheepishly, shrugging my shoulder at Luna's glare.

"And yet, here we are today with a dead body and I'm the last to know what's going on," Luna said, searching through her basket for the perfect French fry.

"Well, not really; Cash is," I said, scrunching my nose up. I was going to be in a world of trouble when he found out about this.

"When does he get back from Miami?" Luna asked.

"This afternoon."

"Perfect. Let's double date tonight," Luna said with a

smile. She was currently dating a delightfully delicious urgent-care doctor who seemed to have no issues with Luna's otherworldly powers. Unlike my man.

Okay, maybe that wasn't fair. Cash had always been understanding of what I did for a living. He just took issue with the fact that I often found myself in dangerous situations.

"I'm not certain we need to drag Mathias into all this, either. I'm thinking the fewer people who know about it, the better. It's obvious that whoever is after this stone is willing to kill for it."

"I don't get it though." Miss Elva leaned back and took a sip of her tea. "Why kill the professor now? Why not wait until he's recovered the stone, then steal it from him and kill him then? Wouldn't that make more sense?"

It was a good question. We sat in silence for a moment as we contemplated it.

"Maybe they just wanted his maps?" I asked, dipping another fry in ketchup.

"But still. If they were willing to kill – why not just let someone else do the hard work and then take the bounty? Doesn't make all that much sense," Trace said.

"Unless there was something in the maps they needed or wanted," Miss Elva mused.

"I don't like the sound of this at all," Luna said.

"Well, I think we need to look at the calling card, so to speak. Why was an Aztec snake drawn on the wall? I think that's going to lead us to more answers. Are there, like,

Aztec gangs or something?" I snorted. I couldn't help it. It was kind of a ridiculous thought – that long-lost Aztec gang members were walking around offing people.

"Well, it's actually not that far out of the picture. There's probably somewhere around a million people who still speak Nahautl, what's thought to have been the primary Aztec language," Miss Elva pointed out, and I looked at her in surprise. Why was I always caught off guard by the knowledge that came out of this woman?

"Well, then," I said, slightly miffed.

"Yeah, didn't you pay attention in history class? Just because the Aztec empire fell doesn't mean there aren't descendants," Trace pointed out.

"Well, excuuuuuse me. I must've missed that particular chapter in the book," I said, giving Trace the stink eye.

"It's okay, sweets. It's not easy to remember another country's history. I certainly don't recall it all," Luna said soothingly, and I shot her a smile. "But, what Miss Elva is saying rings true. There very well could be someone with links to the Aztec empire who is after this... godstone."

"Godstone. I suppose that's one way to describe it," I said.

"What do we know about El Serpiente again?" Luna asked, holding up her hand to tick off points on her fingers. "It's an emerald. It's as large as an ostrich egg. It's rumored to have been worn by Quetzalcoatl himself. It was stolen from an ancient temple. It's presumed to have been used by various rulers in many a ritual throughout the years. Yeah, I'd say it's a godstone. Can you imagine the amount of power that stone has absorbed over the years? Especially as the Aztecs were known for ritual human sacrifice. You know as well as I do the type of power that death magick brings – and for all we know the stone could've absorbed the souls as well."

We all paused at that thought.

"This *is* bad," Trace said.

My phone rang from my purse across the room and I jumped up. Hank hopped down and followed me across the room – my little shadow.

"Hello?" I answered, not recognizing the number.

"This is your ADT Security System calling to report a breach."

My breath caught in my throat.

"A breach?"

"I'll have to ask you for your security code before we give any more details."

I rattled off my security code and waited, turning to look at the table, where the others had gone quiet.

"Thank you. Yes, it looks like the back sliding door has been compromised. Are you at home at the moment?"

"No, I'm not."

"Well, I can confirm a breach of the back door. The police have been notified and are on the way. Will you meet them there?"

"Yes, I will. Thank you."

I turned to look at the table.

"They found me already. There's been a break-in at the house." I looked at Miss Elva. "Unless you forgot to lock the back door?"

"Child, I didn't even use the back door. I came in the front and grabbed Hank. Something told me to bring him with me; now I'm glad I did."

My heart skipped a beat and I immediately knelt to the floor and wrapped my arms around Hank. If he had been home…

I shook my head clear of any bad thoughts.

"I have to meet the police there."

"We'll all go. Take the Jeep," Trace said.

That lump the size of Texas was back in my throat, and I could only nod.

Chapter Eight

"So we meet again," Chief Thomas said from where he stood on my front porch.

"We've really got to stop meeting like this," I replied, my joke falling flat as Chief Thomas just shook his head at me.

"I see you've brought the team," Chief Thomas said as he gestured to my friends piled in the Jeep.

"Yeah, we're kind of like the Scooby Doo gang," I said, cracking another joke, then shook my head at myself and held up a hand to stop Chief Thomas from replying. "I'm sorry. I'm upset about this morning and now hearing this – well, I tend to make bad jokes when I'm nervous."

"I can tell you it's not that bad, though I'm surprised they were able to shatter your sliding glass door."

"Shatter?" My voice rose on the last note.

"It doesn't look like they got too far before the alarm

sounded, though."

I walked to the front door and pulled my key out, unlocking the door and pushing it open. Turning, I yelled to Miss Elva, "Keep Hank in the car. There's broken glass everywhere."

Chief Thomas had been right when he said they'd shattered the back door. It looked like a bomb had gone off – shards of glass were strewn across my whole first floor.

"I'm so confused. Aren't those doors supposed to be shatterproof? Don't they just sort of spiderweb crack? You know?" I asked Chief Thomas, shaking my head in bewilderment. I'd chosen those doors specifically for their safety rating.

"That's what I'm saying. It's almost like they used a battering ram." Chief Thomas shook his head, a concerned look on his face.

"A battering ram? Lovely," I said, taking a step into the house and then turning to look at the Chief. "Am I allowed in here?"

"Yes, just don't touch anything."

A police officer was taking photos of my door – well, what was left of it – and the surrounding damage. My gaze raced over my first floor – one large, wide open room with conversation nooks – and I blew out a sigh of relief when I saw that much of my art and collectibles had been left untouched.

"Apparently a neighbor heard the glass shatter and

called at the same time we got the ADT call," Chief Thomas said, coming to stand next to me. "Which is why, I'm assuming, not much was damaged."

"What kind of burglar is willing to make that much noise mid-day?" Luna said from behind me, stepping inside to wrap her arm around my waist. I leaned into her for a moment, her question causing fear to knot in my gut.

"Luna," Chief Thomas nodded his hello at her.

"Someone who has nothing to fear," I murmured and Chief Thomas raised an eyebrow at me.

"Know someone like that?"

"I can only assume it's the same person from this morning," I said, walking across the room to look see if anything had been stolen.

"You'll want to get a door repairman in here asap. Especially as we don't know who did it. Your safety is compromised," Chief Thomas said.

"On it," Luna said, pulling out her cellphone and striding towards the front room. Say what you will about Luna's perfect wardrobe and delicate build – she's a bulldog in crisis situations.

"Can I clean up the glass? Also, if I can't get someone in here to fix the door, I suppose I'll have to pack up my valuables," I murmured, surprised to feel tears fill my eyes. It's a violation to have your personal space broken into, and my usual cocky armor suddenly felt like it had a chink in it.

"Miss Elva said to let you know she's going to set up a

protection spell," a voice whispered in my ear and I jumped, glaring over my shoulder at the spot where Rafe, Miss Elva's pirate ghost, hovered.

"What's wrong?" Chief Thomas asked; he couldn't see Rafe.

"Nothing. A fly buzzed by my ear," I said quickly, moving to the counter to rip a paper towel off the roll and dab at my eyes.

"A fly! As if. The most glorious pirate to ever sail the seven seas, more like it!" Rafe shouted, posing dramatically, and it took all my willpower not to snort.

"Door guys will be here in an hour with three different sizes of doors," Luna said, sizing up my doorframe. "That is a fairly standard-size sliding door, right?"

"Yes, it is. Thank you," I smiled at Luna gratefully.

"Boss, take a look at this," a cop called from the back yard, and I felt the hair on the back of my neck stand up. Luna and I immediately followed Chief Thomas outside, tiptoeing gingerly over the glass and through the large hole in the door.

"My fence!" I exclaimed.

"Why didn't you say something about this right away?" Chief Thomas asked the other officer.

"I dunno. I just thought it was some of her whackadoodle art and psychic crap. But I remembered you mentioning something like this from the murder this morning..." the man trailed off as his eyes landed on us.

Luna and I made identical pictures, hands on hips,

heads tilted as we looked at the officer in disbelief.

"Whackadoodle?" Luna demanded.

"Psychic crap?" I asked.

"Errrm, uh…" The cop scratched his head and looked at Chief Thomas helplessly.

"Jim, why don't you head back to the station and get those photos loaded on the computer, then get a file started," Chief Thomas said kindly, and the man hightailed it around the corner of my house.

"Nice guy," Luna snapped, and Chief Thomas smiled at her.

"Sorry about him. Jim's a fairly small-minded guy. Good at his job though."

"Well, this is certainly none of my whackadoodle art, that's for sure," I said, striding across the lawn to my privacy fence. I'd painted it a deep maroon when I'd moved in and I loved it. But now, white spray paint marred the wood – the drawing an almost exact replica of the one we'd seen on the wall in the motel this morning.

"What the hell are they doing coming after me? I don't even know anything," I griped.

"Who is 'they'?" Luna asked.

"I don't know. Clearly the same person or group that killed the professor this morning. And now they think I know something and I don't."

I whirled around and shouted over the fence. "Hear that? I don't know anything! I don't have your information!"

"Nobody's there," Rafe said helpfully, sitting on top of the fence and picking at his teeth.

"Bite me, Rafe," I seethed, and Chief Thomas looked at me in confusion.

"Chief, do you have any leads?" Luna jumped in smoothly, sending me a look.

"Not so far. We've barely had time to gather evidence before this happened. In fact, right now our leads are Althea and Trace." Chief Thomas looked at me. "Don't take any sudden trips, okay? I'll need you down at the station later today for your statement."

"I'll be there. I'd like to wait for the door guys."

Chief Thomas waved at me as he went around the house. "Get secured up here. I'll arrange for an extra officer to patrol your neighborhood for a while."

"Thank you."

Once alone, Luna and I looked at each other.

"I don't like this."

"You're coming to stay with me," Luna decided.

"Maybe. Let's see what type of protections Miss Elva can set up. In the meantime – feel like painting?"

Luna sighed and looked down at her dress.

"Got an old t-shirt?"

Chapter Nine

Later that day, I snuggled up with Hank on one of my favorite couches – a bright red number tucked into the corner under a suit of armor. I was tired to the bone, yet too antsy and anxious to actually drift off into a nap.

It certainly didn't stop Hank from snoring gently beside me – his tummy facing up and his paws sprawled out.

True to their word, the door guys had arrived within the hour and I'd had a new door in just as much time. Not that I necessarily felt any safer – at least not until Miss Elva reassured me that she'd set a protection spell on the property.

Which basically meant that anyone who crossed the invisible barrier with intent to harm me was going to get a really big zap. It wouldn't necessarily stop anyone – but her wards would sound and I'd be notified before they ever made it to a door or window.

It was something, at least.

I'd then spent almost two hours at the station with Chief Thomas and Trace, going over details while Hank kept the station secretary company.

I jumped as my phone rang and Hank rolled to open one eye in a glare.

"Cash," I said into the phone, reading his name from the caller ID. I immediately felt guilty for not telling him about my day.

"Hey sweets, I just wanted to touch base with you. How did your dives go on your big expedition today?"

His voice – like whiskey-soaked honey – warmed me and I wished he were near enough to curl up into.

"Well, about that," I said, my voice cracking before I paused.

"Why do I feel like I'm not going to like what comes next?" Cash asked on a sigh.

"Oh, you're not," I said and launched into the story, the words flooding out of me and crowding each other as I tried to get through all the details.

"Wait just a minute – the house got broken into and you didn't call me?" Cash asked, a note of disbelief in his voice.

"I… it all happened so fast, and then I had to go to the station and give a statement. Then I was on the phone with my insurance. And I'm just sitting down. I swear I was going to call you," I said, running my hand over Hank's belly.

"You know, most girls would call their boyfriend right away," Cash said, annoyance lacing his voice.

"It was a crazy day, Cash. Plus I knew you were in meetings all day," I said, hating the plaintive note creeping into my voice. *I* was the victim here, wasn't I? The male ego, I tell ya.

"Well, I suppose you didn't need me since Trace was there," Cash said, working himself into a good head of mad.

"Hey, now. It wasn't like that. Luna, Beau, Trace, and Miss Elva were all here. It wasn't like it was just Trace and me," I defended myself.

"Oh, so you *did* have time to call the whole crew – just not me."

I stopped, caught.

"I called them because they were *here*. And because Miss Elva was letting Hank out today."

"I see. So as long as I'm in town, I'm okay to call for help? But if I'm not in town then you forget all about me."

Okay, so maybe Cash was seriously pissed.

"Please understand where I'm coming from. It's been a long and scary day. I saw a murdered body. Blood was everywhere," I hiccuped as tears welled up. "My house was broken into. It has been a *very* bad day."

Silence greeted me and I clutched the phone against my head, wiping a tear away with a knuckle.

"I get it. It's just… frustrating. I hate being the last person to know when you're hurting. I'm supposed to be the one who makes things better, okay?"

Well, then. How was I supposed to argue with that?

"I promise to call you in the future," I said.

"Well, let's hope something like this doesn't happen in the future. Though things do seem to happen to you with surprisingly regularity," Cash said.

That burned. Prior to the last six months or so, I'd led a fairly calm life. Not a normal one, by any means, but certainly a non-life-threatening one.

"It's not like this is the status quo for me. I'm not a freakin' detective or something, who's always in the line of fire. These things are an anomaly."

"Well, I don't like it," Cash said.

There it was. What was I supposed to say to that? It wasn't as if I liked being in danger either.

"Well, I guess it's all about you, then," I said, my temper rising.

Cash sighed.

"I'm not coming down until tomorrow. I was calling to tell you I'm bringing my sister. She wants to meet you and Beau."

Well, shit.

"I'm not sure if this is a very good time," I said, and not least because I wasn't sure I was ready to meet another member of Cash's family, who were all wildly successful and practically perfect. At least from what I'd heard.

"Too late. I'm at the airport picking her up. Unless you'd prefer we stay in Miami for the rest of her time off?"

THREE TEQUILAS

"I – uh, no. Of course not. Will she be staying at my house?"

"I booked her a room so we can have some space. I know you like your space," Cash said, and I breathed a sigh of relief. "Plus she needs some room to spread out and do a little work. Even though she's on vacation, she's not really *on vacation,* you know?"

Cash's sister was a copyeditor for Vogue, if you can believe that. Not only did she rarely take vacation days, but pictures of her showed that she had certainly inherited her share of the good looks that ran in Cash's family. I was already intimidated.

"I'm sure Farah will find she can relax here in Tequila Key. It's hard not to."

"You can take the New Yorker out of New York..." Cash laughed and I released a breath, some of the tension that had knotted my shoulders easing.

"When will you guys get down here?"

"Probably mid-afternoon. Want to eat dinner at Lucky's? That way she can meet Beau too."

"Sure, I'll warn him. Sure you don't want to try his new restaurant? He'd probably open it early just to impress Farah."

"Nah, I know he's in the final throes of construction and finishing touches. I like Lucky's. Farah will too."

I wasn't so sure about that, but I let it slide.

"See you tomorrow," I said.

"Stay safe. And call me if anything happens," Cash ordered.

"Will do."

We hung up without saying "I love you." We hadn't quite progressed to that stage of our relationship yet. It was hard to really know my feelings for Cash. In fact, I'm not sure I'd ever really been in love. I was naturally suspicious of love, though I had no reason to be. My parents had the type of relationship every couple wished for. They doted on each other, celebrated the weird in each other, and traveled the world together.

So why was I keeping my feelings for Cash hidden behind a wall?

The little voice in my head told me why.

I was convinced I wasn't good enough for Cash and his fancy family. And sooner or later, he was going to realize that being with a tattooed psychic like me did not fall in line with his family's plan for a house in upstate Connecticut and grandkids running on the lawn.

I sighed and pinched my nose. That wasn't fair of me. Cash had never once made me feel like I wasn't good enough for him. In fact, he treated me better than I'd ever been taken care of before. It was my own insecurities that were sabotaging my feelings for him.

What would my mother say?

As if on cue, my phone rang and I glanced down to see my mother's name on the display. I wondered what part of the world she was in now.

"Darling…can you hear me? It's dreadfully windy

here," Abigail called through the phone. I winced at her loud voice.

"Loud and clear, Mom. How are you?" I asked brightly, curling into a pillow on the couch and missing her and my father.

"Positively delightful. The diving has been to die for. You must come here sometime. With the photos you take? Darling, you'll be a sensation!"

I smiled into the phone. I loved my mother – she was my constant champion.

"How's Dad doing?"

"He's ecstatic. He's been jamming with one of the musicians on the boat. A Jack Johnson – John Johnson? I'm not quite sure. Oh, and I've given some marvelous readings."

"Jack Johnson, Mom. He's quite famous."

"Well, I would hope so, if he can afford the yacht we're on." She chuckled, then paused before continuing, "Now, I had a vision today, which is why I'm calling."

Abigail's visions were not to be dismissed.

"Is something going on there? I feel like you're in danger and I'm quite worried."

I filled her in quickly, sketching out the details. Her sharp intake of breath said it all.

"El Serpiente. That was my vision. A snake with glowing emerald green eyes. It was arched back, ready to bite your neck. Please, oh please be careful on this mission of yours."

"I don't think there is a mission anymore. The professor is dead. So the expedition is probably over." I shrugged, though her words chilled me.

"Althea, you've discovered your magick, haven't you?"

"Luna is teaching me, yes. Though she wants to have a few choice words with you," I said, biting back my annoyance at my mom's glossing over of the little tidbit that I had magick on top of my psychic abilities.

"Yes, well, it wasn't time. Now it's time. I'd like you to ask Luna to teach you the locator spell. It can be used inversely as well. In fact, I insist upon it."

"Used inversely? I'm not sure what that means."

"Althea… I can't hear you. I think the connection is bad. I love you. Promise to email me daily!"

Then the connection was lost and I sat there staring down at the phone.

Sliding through the screens, I pulled up Luna's name and texted her what my mother had told me.

"Meet me at the shop in the morning. I'll call Miss Elva."

It looked like I was going to have another magick lesson whether I liked it or not.

"Come on, Hank. Let's go snuggle in bed and forget about this day."

But I left every light in the house burning. Just in case.

Chapter Ten

"You'd better have coffee back there. Damn near up before the birds," Miss Elva complained as she swept into the shop, Rafe floating along behind her. Today's caftan was a brilliant pearl white with an intricate turquoise design stitched across it. Her hair was wrapped in a matching turquoise scarf and earrings the size of doorknockers dangled to her shoulders.

"It certainly didn't compromise your style. Unless you sleep in that?" I asked, nodding at her caftan as I handed her a cup of coffee.

Now me? I wouldn't drink coffee if I were wearing a white dress. But to each her own.

"Child, you couldn't handle seeing what I sleep in," Miss Elva chuckled, sending her generous curves rolling. I raised an eyebrow at her.

"It's glorious," Rafe breathed, fluttering around her

head. "My lovemountain sure can fill out some lace."

"Mmmhmm, and don't you forget that, sweetcakes," Miss Elva laughed and sipped her coffee.

"I'm all ready back here," Luna called from her back room.

We were on her side of the shop. We didn't typically open the doors until ten or eleven during the week as foot traffic was fairly slow in the morning hours. I would come in earlier if I had a scheduled appointment, but otherwise those hours worked for us – I got to dive in the mornings and Luna worked on more charms and spells for her products.

A well-sized and well-stocked backroom was tucked off Luna's side of the store. She'd transformed it into one of the prettiest ritual rooms I'd ever had the pleasure of seeing. I mean, did I expect any differently? Anything Luna had her hand in was pure elegance.

"Now, child, did I hear you correctly? Your mama wants you to learn a locator spell?" Miss Elva asked, placing her coffee on a low table as she went to examine the items Luna had placed on the ritual table set outside the circle drawn on the floor.

"That's what she said. And that it can be used inversely," I said, shrugging.

"To find and be found," Miss Elva said.

"That's advanced magick. I can't even get her to properly cast a circle," Luna complained. "Now Abigail wants me to teach her a locator spell? She needs to get her psychic butt back here and bestow some of her *own* wisdom on her daughter."

"Amen," Miss Elva and I said at the same time.

Luna huffed out a laugh and then shrugged.

"I love her, but damn it, she's dropped a load on us."

"Is this, like, super hard to learn?"

"It's not even necessarily hard to learn – it's just that when you need to use it, you'll most likely be stressed or under duress. So that means you'll need to clearly remember the spell. If you mix it up, who knows?"

"Who knows? What the hell, Luna?"

"Well? What do you want me to say? Who knows means just that… who knows? If you do the spell wrong, you might be led in a wrong direction. Magick is a picky thing. Which is why I'm annoyed at Abigail."

"Fine, remember the spell precisely. Got it. Let's get started. The more we go over it, the easier it will be for me to remember it."

Miss Elva and Luna looked at each other across the circle.

"How do you want to start it?"

"Did you hide something?"

"I did."

"What did you hide?" I looked back and forth between the both of them.

"Herman."

"My skeleton?" I shrieked. I loved my skeleton. He hung out in the corner of my shop, sporting a Ramones shirt. Herman had been with me since I started my business. I'd found him at a thrift shop the same week we opened. Aside from a brief stint where I'd redecorated my shop to look like a lawyer's office – and had subsequently lost business – Herman had maintained his seat on my leopard print chair in the corner.

"You'd better not have hurt him," I complained.

"It's impossible to hurt him. He's made of plastic," Luna pointed out.

"I don't care. He has feelings. I talk to him," I grumbled.

"Focus, Thea. We're going to start with the most basic of locator spells, for finding something you have a connection to. You can use this if you lose your keys, or – goddess forbid – Hank. That kind of thing. A personal or emotional connection."

I nodded for her to continue.

"So, to start out you'll want to clear your mind as best you can. Focus on the object that you're trying to find and – if you can – invoke an emotional connection with it."

I closed my eyes and brought Herman to my mind. And then ruined it by snorting with laughter.

"Sorry," I said, holding my hand up in apology. "I just never much thought about my emotional connection to Herman."

"Just focus, Althea. This shouldn't be so difficult," Luna complained.

"Fine, fine, I'm focusing."

I did, too – closed my eyes and brought Herman in his Ramones t-shirt to my mind.

"Got it? Good, now let's work on a few key components of the spell. The first is intent. As with all spells, your intent must be true – and must be spoken. 'I intend for such and such to happen. I intend to do the following things.' You don't want to leave a lot of grey area when casting a spell or you can find yourself in a world of pain."

"You're entering a world of pain," I joked, quoting Walter from *The Big Lebowski*.

Luna rolled her eyes, but she laughed anyway.

"So, number one – intent. Got it?"

I nodded.

"Yes, I intend to find Herman. Got it."

"Next up is casting your circle and calling on the elements. Last time we did this, you brought Rafe through – so you know the dangers of doing this wrong," Luna said.

"Don't act like you didn't want me to come through. You ladies were dancing naked on a beach – dying for a real man to appear in your lives," Rafe shouted from the front room.

"Rafe, I know you didn't just imply that you are the 'real man' for these two," Miss Elva called over her shoulder.

"No, no – of course not, my lovemountain. It's always you for me. You know that," Rafe crooned.

I shook my head. "Moving on."

"So you'll want to call on the elements."

"What if she's not in a position to cast a circle?" Miss Elva asked.

"Well, that's what I'm saying – then she can just invoke the elements without the circle," Luna pointed out.

"Yeah, let's just teach her that. If we're going to be totally honest here, you know she's only going to use magick when she's in a total bind – and that means there's gonna be no time for circle casting."

"Fine, we'll do modified," Luna said, then turned to me with a bright smile on her face, like a teacher who had the painful job of teaching the slowest student in the class. "Okay, Thea, repeat after me."

"Repeat after me," I parroted back, and she scrunched her nose at me.

"Focus."

"Focus," I repeated.

Miss Elva snorted. "Someone's got her sassy pants on today."

"Fine, fine, go ahead," I sighed.

"By the moon, sun, earth, air, fire, and sea,

What once was lost, now returns to me."

I repeated the phrase back to her while keeping Herman in my mind. Soon, a soft glow appeared in my mind.

"I swear I see a little light," I said, closing my eyes as I focused on it.

"Follow it," Luna instructed.

"With my mind or physically?"

"Depends. What does your gut say?"

"In this instance, I think I'll follow it physically," I said, and closed my eyes again to get a reading on the light. Opening them, I left the backroom and walked through Luna's store, the light growing stronger in my mind. Opening the front door, I paused and turned my head, looking around until I located the glow. In moments, I stood at the back of Luna's Mini, the light in my mind all but blinking frenetically. Reaching down, I popped the back open to find Herman, his arms curled around a plush panda bear toy, looking up at me from the trunk.

"Caught in the act!" Miss Elva chuckled from the porch, shaking her head down at Herman. "You may want to leave those two alone. Looks like they're getting to know each other better."

I glared at Miss Elva. "Herman doesn't even like pandas."

"You don't know that," Luna chuckled. "Sure looks like he does from here."

Finally, I laughed and pulled Herman from the trunk and threw him over my shoulder. Seizing the panda as well, I looked up at Luna.

"Herman's keeping the panda. Your loss."

"Fair enough." Luna smiled as I sailed past her towards the store and into the side that housed my shop. Plopping Herman back on the leopard print chair, I tucked the panda into his lap, looping one of his arms around it.

I hated to admit it, but he did look marginally happier with the panda on his lap.

"Okay, so you wanted a buddy. Now you have one."

Did I mention that my life is not a normal one? As I stood there talking to a plastic skeleton, I could only imagine what the members of Cash's family would think. They were probably all at their high-powered office jobs, holding meetings and signing contracts.

Well, I held meetings too.

Our clients were just decidedly different, was all.

Chapter Eleven

An hour later, Miss Elva and Luna had put me through my paces and I felt like I was well versed in the locator spell. I moved to my shop to open the screen so Hank could bounce over into Luna's side of the store. I hadn't been able to leave him at home this morning, what with the safety issues and all. I don't think I'd be able to live through something happening to Hank.

"Devil beast!" Rafe hissed and zoomed across the room to hide behind Miss Elva's shoulder.

Hank, sensing it was playtime, ran across the store and barked up at Rafe, his rump shaking back and forth in excitement. Hank really liked to rile up the ghost.

"Call him off!"

"Rafe, we've been over this. You know he won't hurt you. He just likes to play."

"Give him the skeleton to play with. Dogs like bones,

I hear." Rafe peeked over Miss Elva's shoulder and looked down at Hank.

Hank gave one short, sharp bark and Rafe ducked again.

"For such a mean take-no-prisoners pirate, you sure are afraid of a tiny little dog," I laughed at Rafe, and he popped his head up to glare at me.

"I fear nothing!"

Hank barked again and ran behind Miss Elva, causing Rafe to shriek and fly across the room. A game of chase ensued, and we all dissolved into fits of laughter while Rafe freaked out.

"The beast! Call him off!"

Hank cornered Rafe on a table, dancing below him with his tongue lolling out.

"Hank, buddy, come here. I've got a treat for you," I said, pulling a treat from my purse and giving Rafe a break.

"Stupid devil beast," Rafe muttered, slinking back to Miss Elva's side.

"Now honey-bear, I told you that dog just wants to play. You need to not give them so much ammo to laugh at you," Miss Elva soothed. "Hank's just a sweet doll baby who wants to have fun."

"I don't trust it," Rafe insisted.

"Try not flying around so much, and maybe he won't chase you," Miss Elva said.

The door to Luna's shop swung open with a bang and we all jumped. Hank immediately ran across the room to investigate.

"Trace?" I asked, surprised to see him standing in the doorway. And then I took in his appearance. His lip was cut and his right eye was almost completely swollen shut.

"What happened?" We all gasped at once, while I rushed across the room to grab his arm and drag him inside to a pretty loveseat tucked in an alcove of Luna's store.

I sat next to him and immediately reached out to turn his face towards me so I could examine his wounds.

"I'm fine," Trace said bitterly, pushing my hand away.

Have I mentioned the male ego? Yeah, it's annoying.

"You're not fine. You're clearly hurt and I want to see your bruises," I said, annoyed with him. Trace turned to look at me, but made no comment when I ran my hands through his hair, testing for any other lumps or scrapes.

Let's be honest, all men like to be fussed over. Even when they pretend they don't. I swear, a man gets a cold and it's like the world is ending. More serious injuries than that? Well, we all knew Trace would want us to cluck over him.

And cluck over him we did. Luna brought a glass of water and some Advil, Miss Elva ran her hands over his arms, testing for any internal injuries, and Hank licked his hand. When we were all satisfied that nothing more was amiss, we sat back to hear what had happened.

"I interrupted someone trying to break in last night. They knocked me out, though I'm not proud to admit that. But they did – then I awoke to this," Trace pulled a card out of his pocket – about the size of a playing card – and turned it over to show the same Aztec snake drawing we had seen twice before.

"You were knocked out while they were there?" I gasped.

"Yeah, my house got tossed. I spent the morning with Chief Thomas going over everything. The only thing taken was my laptop."

"You didn't call me," I said, shocked and a little hurt that he hadn't reached out to any of us.

"I had a lot going on. I'm telling you now," Trace shrugged it off and I tamped down my annoyance. After all, I'd been guilty of the same thing yesterday with Cash, hadn't I?

"What would they want with your laptop?"

"I'm assuming they were after some of the coordinates for the dive sites," Trace said, leaning back and closing his eyes.

"Did you have those? You didn't tell me."

"I didn't. The professor alluded to a few areas. But he never gave up the actual coordinates. Only said we'd discuss it once we were out on the boat."

"Here, child, let me fix you up," Miss Elva said, motioning for me to move from the loveseat. I bit my lip and watched as Miss Elva laid her hands on Trace's face, murmured a few words, and then eased the bruises from his face. In a matter of moments, the swelling was gone and

Trace was looking at Miss Elva with a bemused expression on his face.

"I could marry you. Thank you," Trace said, leaning over and planting a light kiss on Miss Elva's lips.

"He dares! To touch! My woman!" Rafe screeched, startling all of us as he flew at Trace. Trace, oblivious to the ghost, shivered as Rafe rushed through him.

"Rafe, knock it off," Miss Elva said mildly and Trace looked around.

"What?"

"Nothing, let's stay focused here. So, we're clearly being targeted," I said, returning to the important topic.

"We're being targeted, that's for sure."

"So what do you do?" Luna asked, looking back and forth between us.

I met Trace's eyes.

We spoke at the same time. "We have to find the treasure first."

Luna threw up her hands in disgust.

"Well, it's obvious y'all have a death wish."

Chapter Twelve

"It just makes sense," I argued with Luna.

"How in the world does it make sense? The professor was murdered because they thought he might *know* about the treasure. What do you think is going to happen when you actually *have* the treasure?" Luna demanded, her hands on her hips.

"Oh, did someone say treasure?" Rafe asked, his eyes lighting up with glee. I'm assuming that treasure to a pirate is like mint-chocolate chip ice cream to me when I'm PMSing.

We ignored Rafe.

"Listen, if we find the treasure and turn it in to a museum or something, then we'll be off the hook."

"Can't we just find the guy who's killing people and turn *him* in? Wouldn't that make more sense?" Luna asked.

I shook my head.

"If there's one, there's more. We've got to find the treasure."

"I remember some of the areas the prof was talking about. Even though he wasn't exact, it was hard for him to explain what he wanted without giving me some sense of direction. I'm sure I could at least get us started. Plus, if we spend some time studying the route the treasure fleet took, I suspect we can follow the paths of some of the more recent hurricanes and see where ships tend to end up. I think we could begin to narrow in on an area to start in."

"Treasure fleet – why, I know…" Rafe began.

"I'm glad to hear that. You're precisely the person I've been looking for."

We all jumped at the melodic English accent that wafted towards us from the door. As if on cue, we turned as one to see a dainty young woman with sandy blonde hair and an honest-to-god pillbox hat on her head standing in the still-open door of Luna's shop.

"Trace? And, I'm presuming, Althea? I'm Nicola, Professor Johansson's niece."

"That there's a nice hat, honey," Miss Elva observed.

Chapter Thirteen

"Oh, well, yes, thank you. I know you Americans aren't terribly fond of hats, but it's hard to break the habit, I suppose," Nicola said as she touched her hat gently.

"I don't know about that. I like a nice hat. Though I really prefer fascinators myself. I think it just completes an outfit, you know?" Miss Elva and Nicola looked at each other in mutual accord.

I did not like this woman. That was literally my first thought, and I had no idea why. But years of being a psychic have taught me to trust my instincts.

"I thought hats were on their way out. Aren't you a little young to be wearing that trend?"

Nicola raised an eyebrow at me.

"A hat is always in style."

Well, then. I guess I knew where I stood.

"I'm sorry about your uncle," I said, deciding to start

over with this girl.

"Yes, well, we are all distraught, of course."

I blinked at her. A less distraught person than this girl I had yet to see, impeccably buttoned-up as she was, with not a hair out of place and no makeup smudges under her eyes from crying.

"Sure don't look like you've been up all night crying or anything," Miss Elva said, crossing her arms over her considerable chest.

Bless you, Miss Elva.

"Ah, the British stiff upper lip and that. One must always save face."

What she said was true – yet I decided I'd be keeping a close eye on this one.

"You said you were looking for Trace. How did you know to find him here?"

"It wasn't terribly hard. I stopped at his boat and when I saw that it was docked, I went down the list of names of people my uncle was working with. Althea's was next on the list, and this was listed as her place of business. I'm assuming you are Althea?" Nicola looked directly at me.

"Why do you think I'm Althea?" I asked, crossing my own arms over my chest. Nicola sighed and pinched the bridge of her nose.

"Are you Althea Rose, the underwater photographer and – judging from this shop," Nicola looked around and sniffed, "also a psychic?"

Did that bitch just sniff at my shop? I lifted my lip in a near-snarl, but Luna put her hand on my arm and stepped forward.

"Actually, this side of the shop is mine. I'm Luna. So... *interesting* to meet you. I'm surprised you were able to make it from London so quickly."

That was an excellent point.

"Yeah, you must have hopped on the first plane out upon hearing the news," I said, doing the math in my head. It would have taken quite a bit to get here this early in the day after news made it back to London. And this girl had not a single dark circle under her eyes. "But you don't look very tired," I finished.

"Are you Americans always so suspicious of people?" Nicola asked, her temper beginning to show. I kind of wanted to push her, just to see where it would take us. People reveal all sorts of interesting things about themselves when they lose their tempers.

"I'm Trace, this is Althea, and Miss Elva, and Luna," Trace said, standing and coming forward to shake Nicola's hand. She immediately twinkled up at him and I groaned. Hank snorted and didn't bother going to greet Nicola which immediately caused me to raise an eyebrow.

"Here we go," I mumbled to Miss Elva, and she snorted.

"Lovely to meet you, really, just a delight," Nicola cooed, and I think all of the women in the room collectively rolled their eyes at the same time.

"Are you here to take the body home?"

"Er... no, actually, I'm here to continue the expedition."

"What expedition?" I cut off whatever Trace was about to say, and even though he shot me a quick look, I think he realized what I was trying to do.

Nicola looked around, then stepped in closer to the rest of us.

"Well, you know. The expedition to find El Serpiente."

Miss Elva sucked in a breath and clucked her tongue. "Child, I'd be real careful about where you drop that name around this town."

Nicola looked startled for a moment and then her features smoothed out.

"Of course, you're right. I do understand the confidential nature of this project."

"Do you understand the dangers as well?" I couldn't help but pick at her. Something about her absolutely precise nature bothered me.

"My uncle was just murdered in cold blood. I'm well aware of the dangers," Nicola said dryly. I felt my lip curl up in disgust again.

"Well, best of luck to you on finding what you're looking for. I've got work to see to," I said, deciding then and there that I was having nothing to do with Miss Priss. I gave Nicola my patented polite 'screw you' smile and breezed into my side of the shop. The last thing I was going to be doing was helping this Nicola chick out of a bind. There were already enough warning signs from the universe, thankyouverymuch.

"Thea."

"Trace, don't even," I began, turning to look at him as he crossed to sit in the client's chair across from me. I shuffled a pack of tarot cards out of habit.

"Going to give me a reading?"

"You can't afford me," I said, a bitchy smile on my face.

"I can if we take this job," Trace smirked back at me, appreciating my bitchiness. That was something I liked about Trace – my being a brat to him never put him off all that much.

"She's offering us an additional $25,000 if we complete the expedition and help her find who murdered her uncle," Trace said softly, his gaze holding mine.

"That's nice of her. No."

"Aw, come on, Althea. We were going to hunt for the treasure anyway. Might as well make some extra cash on top of it."

"Nope. I'm good," I said, shaking my head at Trace.

"Well, I know you're good. But I'm not. I still have student loans I'm paying off. And it would be nice to buy a little place down here instead of renting," Trace pointed out.

Shit. I'm a sucker for a guilt trip.

I narrowed my eyes at him and then glanced at Luna's

side of the shop. Trace had pulled my privacy screen closed and I was certain Luna and Miss Elva would distract Nicola.

"I don't trust her."

"You don't have to trust her to work for her," Trace said.

"On an expedition like this? Um, yeah, I do," I said.

"Come on, Thea. Think about it – we know the water, we know the boat, we know diving. She doesn't. She's the one who's out of her element here. Not us. We've got the upper hand."

"What about the psycho going around killing people?"

"He's doing that already. Who says this'll make it any worse? I've got a feeling it's not going to stop until the treasure is found."

"Someone else can find it, and we can stay clear of it."

Trace leveled a look at me. "Is that really what you want to do?"

"No, I want to find the treasure," I admitted. Damn it, but apparently I also had an excited child deep inside me who was desperate to go on a treasure hunt.

"So?"

My mind was working furiously. "Here's the deal," I finally said. "A hundred grand, half up front and non-refundable, plus we get a twenty percent share of the value of any treasure. I retain copyright of my images, she pays for all trip costs – gas, food, etc. – and we arrange for a GPS locator signal and tracking by the Coast Guard or

Chief Thomas."

I couldn't believe I was agreeing to this. I had to have lost my damn mind. Cash was going to be furious with me.

Trace let out a low whistle.

"Driving a hard bargain, are we?"

"A man's already dead. It's the only bargain I'll take."

"I can't see her agreeing to the tracking signal; this is supposed to be a private expedition," Trace pointed out.

"It's your boat. Put one on anyway."

"Then how about we don't say anything about that aspect of it at all?"

Finally in agreement, I nodded at him.

"Go do your work. Tell British out there to get some sunscreen, too. She's going to fry out on the water."

Chapter Fourteen

"This is a highly unusual contract," Nicola repeated later in the day, scanning the documents my attorney had thrown together for us at my request. Thank goodness for my mother the psychic and her crack team of lawyers – they were used to unusual legal requests.

"We won't help you until the contract is signed and the deposit wired to our accounts," I said sweetly, sipping my iced coffee and watching her. She still had that stupid hat on.

"I can read," Nicola said, raising a perfectly manicured eyebrow at me.

"I'm sorry. Naturally we're a little on edge, after your uncle's death and all. There seems to be more at stake here than we realized," Trace said gently, leaving an opening for Nicola to tell us more.

"Yes, well, we certainly must find the treasure now. I

wouldn't want Uncle's death to be in vain," Nicola said, spitting out the words.

"Nicola, what is it that you do? Why would the expedition investor even send you to investigate this? Are you in the same line of work?"

"I'm an auctioneer, actually, so I've quite the extensive background in antiquities and history," Nicola said, her accent heightening the snootiness in her tone. I wanted to reach over and pluck the hat off her head and toss it on the ground. Instead, I smiled at her.

"So this investor has hired you to finish the job?"

"Correct."

Quite the talker, this one.

"Who is the investor?"

"It's a silent investor who's chosen to remain anonymous. The only information I have is the name of our contact, Quetz Investments." Nicola shrugged.

"So you have no issue whatsoever with blindly following the search for a lost treasure, one which cost your uncle his life, on behalf of an investor that you know nothing about?" I asked.

"For what they are paying me? Absolutely. And, it's still through the Institute. They have authorized the expedition, and it's not as if they're some backyard mercenary salvage company." Nicola laughed as though the idea was the funniest thing in the world.

"See, Althea? That's a little more comforting, right? The Institute is still heading up the expedition," Trace said, passing me a scone.

We were back at Beanz, drinking iced coffees – tea for Nicola, of course – and eating scones while lazy tourists wandered past the windows. I'd had more than my normal coffee intake for the day and the jitters were taking over, making me bitchier than usual.

"I want to make this very clear," I said quietly, leaning over until Nicola dropped the contract and met my eyes. "If at any time I sense any bullshit or foul play from you, this contract is terminated. We will walk. I'm not stupid and I certainly will not play around with our lives. And if you do anything dumb – like put us in the path of this killer – I will make sure that you are first in line. Understood?"

Nicola stared me down, her brown eyes hard, before she finally nodded.

"Understood."

"You'll see that noted in Clause 18 as well."

I had asked my attorney to add a no-bullshit clause to the contract. Hey, it might not be totally legal, but if they signed it – well, that's on them.

"I'll have to fax this to the Institute. If all goes well, we should be able to leave tomorrow."

"You think they'll have fifty thousand dollars in our bank accounts by tomorrow? Please," I looked at my phone – it was already mid-afternoon.

"Yes," Nicola said simply, rising and tucking the papers into her briefcase. "I'll be in touch."

She swept from the room; her buttoned-up blouse and skirt were in sharp contrast to the flowy beachwear most of the other patrons were wearing. I caught more than one person giving her a look.

"Well, she certainly stands out in a crowd," I said to Trace. I leaned back, trying to see what type of car she got into, but she disappeared around the corner of the building without approaching any of the cars parked on the street in front.

"You were really all over her," Trace said, taking another bite of his scone.

"Well, I'm sorry, but come on. Uncle gets murdered, she doesn't shed a tear, is here the next day to negotiate a new contract with us? And in the meantime both of our houses have been broken into? You don't think this is completely messed up?"

"Well, the British are notorious for not showing their emotions, so I'm not totally put off by that," Trace said.

"Yes, I can see you find her charming," I said dryly, rolling my eyes.

"She's not bad to look at, I'll admit that," Trace said with a grin, "Why, Thea? You jealous?"

"I'm annoyed, is what I am. I don't like being threatened and I certainly think all this is fishy."

"Let's just see how it plays out. We'll stay on guard. I'm armed. You apparently have magick protections on the house. So we lay low, do some research, and see what happens. Either way, we should each have fifty thousand non-refundable dollars in our bank accounts tomorrow. I don't know about you, but that's a lot of money for me."

"It's a lot of money for me too. But I'm worried – I just am."

"Good. That'll keep you on edge. You have a tendency to fall into trouble when your head's in the sky and you aren't paying attention."

Damn it. The man had a point.

"So what do we do now?"

"We wait and we research. I think we need to ask Miss Elva to do some research, too. That woman has scary good connections."

"Cash comes home tonight. I don't think he's going to like this."

"If you were so concerned about that, I don't think you would have written up a new contract to proceed."

Trace was really beginning to annoy me now.

"I'll just see myself out," I mumbled.

His chuckle followed me out the door.

Chapter Fifteen

"He's bringing his sister?" Beau hissed at me over the phone. I could hear the chaos of the kitchen at Lucky's in the background.

"Yes, tonight."

I was standing in front of my closet debating what to wear. I mean, it wasn't just dinner with his sister – it was dinner with his sister the fashion editor.

"And you're just getting around to telling me this *now?*"

"Sorry, long day." I filled him in on the new developments as I pulled dress after dress from the closet.

"Now I have to go home and change," Beau said, zeroing in on the important stuff.

"Tell me about it. She's a fashion editor."

There was a moment of dead silence, followed by a noise like a teakettle emitting steam coming through the phone.

"I'm going to kill Dylan for not telling me."

Dylan, Cash's younger brother, had been dating Beau off and on for a few months now. Between Beau opening a new restaurant and Dylan not living in Tequila Key, they'd kept it fairly loose and open, though I knew Beau would like to see more of Dylan.

"Is Dylan even in town?" I asked, holding up a red shift dress, then discarding it.

"He's not. He'll be back in a couple weeks, though."

"Sorry, babe. I don't know what to tell you. All I know is Cash said he wanted to bring Farah to Lucky's to meet you."

"I've got to run home and change. Shit," Beau said.

"At least you've got good style. What the hell do I wear to meet a fashion editor?"

"Wear that new kimono-sleeved maxi dress I bought you in Miami. The silk one? It's a knockout and flatters all the right areas."

"Ohhhh, I forgot about that one. It hasn't entered my rotation yet." I breathed a sigh of relief. Beau had impeccable taste and knew my sizes – he always brought me back something fun when he went up to the mainland.

"See you later. Text me before you get here," Beau said, hanging up without waiting for my reply.

I pulled the dress from my closet, still in its plastic dress bag. It really was lovely – and I'd been saving it for a date with Cash. A deep red, it was shot through with orange and turquoise accents. It looked exotic and worldly – the sort of thing a woman who knew her own worth would wear.

In fact, it kind of reminded me of Miss Elva.

I drew it from the bag and held it up to myself, studying my reflection in the full length mirror hanging from the back of my closet door.

"Perfect. Right, Hank?"

Hank cocked his head at me from his bed by the bathroom door, where he lay chewing one of his bones.

"I'll take that as a yes. Now to figure out my hair."

Twenty minutes later, I'd gone through my bathroom routine, had taken extra care with my makeup, and had added some new styling cream to my curls. There wasn't much left to do but pick out some earrings and put on my dress. For now, though, I let my curls dry a bit more and waited to hear from Cash.

I sat in my bedside reading chair and grabbed my laptop. It wouldn't hurt to do some more research on El Serpiente while I waited. After our meeting with Nicola earlier today, I'd shot Miss Elva a text with some questions, and she'd promised to email me anything she found. Signing in to my email, I was pleased to see that she had delivered.

"Shut up, a map and everything," I murmured, clicking through the attachments Miss Elva had sent. One image was a map – but it looked like a photograph that someone had taken, not a scanned image of the actual map. Which made me wonder just who Miss Elva had gotten the map from. Scrolling back up, I looked at her email.

Don't ask. And don't share this.

Succinct as always.

From what I could discern, this map was hand-drawn; it looked quite aged – the lettering was an old calligrapher's style and the paper was all but falling apart. I itched to be able to pick it up and use my psychic abilities to get a read on it. But from what I was getting just from the photo? This was the mapped route of the treasure fleet.

And the next image was handwritten documentation – degrees of latitude and all – of all the storms in the Caribbean the summer the treasure fleet had set sail.

"Holy shit. So if we follow their trajectory…" I swore. I really needed Trace for this. He was better at mapping out currents and where the trade winds would take us. I almost hit the forward button – then caught myself.

Trace's laptop had been stolen. Which very well could mean that someone was monitoring his email, if he'd had his email open on his computer. And I'm sure he had – didn't most people? For the sake of convenience?

Instead, I pulled the images up on my iPhone and saved them, making a mental note to print them out later. My phone beeped with an incoming message while it was in my hand.

Contracts approved. Transfer being made. We dive at dawn. Meet me at the boat.

I immediately signed into my bank account and was surprised to see that $5,000 was already in my savings, with the additional $45,000 listed as pending. I knew banks always put a hold on large deposits, so it didn't bother me to see that. Before I even knew it, I was on Nordstrom's Online, cruising through their maxi dress section. Pausing, I shook my head like I was coming out of a fog.

Yeesh, I get one windfall and I'm already shopping for new clothes.

"Come on, Hank, I know you're hungry," I said, sending Hank into a tailspin of ecstatic circles.

Cash called on the way downstairs.

"Hey, babe," I said, deliberately infusing my voice with cheer.

"Hey, cutie, we'll be in Tequila in about twenty minutes or so. Do you want us to pick you up or meet you at the restaurant?"

I thought about it for a moment as I pulled out Hank's dog food bin.

"I'll meet you there. The hotel's on the other side of town anyway."

"Yeah, but I'm not staying at the hotel."

His words sent shivers through me. Damn but he was hot.

"Then I guess I'll see you in a half hour," I said lightly.

"Hank! Time to go outside!" The dog jumped at my shriek and raced towards the back door. I flung it open and watched as he did his business. Usually I'd let him run around outside in the yard by himself, but after the week we'd had I was on high alert.

Miss Elva had explained about the wards she'd put in place around the house – but even knowing Miss Elva and her indomitable powers, I was still nervous. I felt like we were battling some invisible force – an unknown entity – and I didn't like it. Especially because the legend of El Serpiente didn't exactly make me feel all that confident in our venture.

"Good boy," I cooed down to Hank, then went over to my purse. I'd stopped at Fins, the general store in town, and picked up some brand new toys for him today. It wasn't often that he got new toys, as I did like to rotate the ones we already had – but I figured he deserved it for being awesome.

I mean – don't we all deserve gifts for being awesome?

"Check this out, Hank! A treat ball and a new squeaky toy," I said, pulling open the treat ball and putting a portion of his food in the dispenser. The goal was to keep him stimulated – he'd have to nose the ball around to work the food out. Hank tilted his head at the hard plastic ball when I placed it in front of him and then looked at me in confusion. Usually I launched the ball across the room.

"Go on, sniff it," I said, nudging the ball with my toe. As soon as I did, a piece of kibble fell out and Hank pounced. Instantly understanding the game, he began to push the ball around the room, stopping to eat pieces of kibble as they fell out.

I swear he shot me a look of pure joy before going back to the ball.

"Dress," I said, and raced upstairs. Taking my robe off, I pulled the dress over my head, then double-checked to make sure there were no tags on the dress. I tousled up my curls and hung some thick silver hoops from my ears.

Taking one last glance in the mirror, I blew out a breath. This was the best his sister was going to get – and I had to say, I looked fabulous.

"Game on," I murmured.

Chapter Sixteen

I WAS WAITING on my front porch when Cash's Jeep rolled up. In stark contrast to Trace's battered and rusted Jeep, Cash's Jeep gleamed and boasted shiny new rims. Cash immediately got out and rounded the car to open the back door for me – pausing to lean in and slide his lips across mine.

I leaned into his warmth for a second, before pulling back and smiling up at him.

"Good to see you," I said.

Cash was over six feet tall, with dark hair and eyes the color of the sky during a storm. As if that wasn't enough, the man had like zero percent body fat. It was enough to give a girl a complex – when I wasn't too busy being distracted by all the dips and curves of his abs.

"I missed you," Cash said softly, running a finger over my lips before turning and heading back to the driver's side of the car.

"Hi, I'm Althea," I said to Cash's sister as I slid across the back seat. I moved over until I was diagonal from her and offered her my hand.

Of course – she was perfect. I should have expected nothing less – the genes that ran through this family were impeccable.

With dark brown hair cut in a choppy bob that swung around angled cheekbones, her grey eyes perfectly outlined, and wearing jean shorts with a white t-shirt that probably cost more than my dress, Farah was the quintessential effortlessly-cool New York girl. Gold bangles jangled at her wrist as she reached one hand back to shake mine, the other scrolling through her phone. Giving me a cursory glance, she nodded once before returning to whatever she was reading on her phone.

"God, Cash can you believe this? Mom wants us all to go on a family trip. Who has time for that? She's making it mandatory, too. For spouses and significant others. Not that I have anyone to bring."

My stomach turned. A family trip. With significant others? Oh man, there was no way I was ready for that.

"Not like you do either."

Excuse me? What did that bitch just say?

Calm down, my inner peacekeeper urged me. She's testing you, that's all.

"Thank goodness," I said. "Significant others are *so* last year, anyway."

The snark was strong with me today.

"Oh, you don't believe in monogamy then, Althea?" Farah turned and ran her eyes over my outfit, silently letting me know she thought I was way overdressed for going to a casual tiki bar in small-town Tequila Key. I wanted to headbutt her. This was my town – and I'd wear anything I damn well pleased.

"Is that a new religion? I didn't realize it was something to believe in. I'm fairly sure it's a common practice," I said smoothly, already hating this night.

"It doesn't look like you practice much – other than marring your skin," Farah said pointedly, looking at the tattoos that ran up my forearm.

I glanced down at my beautiful Celtic-inspired tattoo with a few little magickal elements worked in. I had even added an evil eye for extra protection. It was a beautiful piece, both delicate in its whimsy and strong in its protection. And this girl had no right to say I had "marred my skin" – I was very proud of my tattoos.

"You'd be amazed at what I practice," I said simply, my eyes meeting Farah's. This had the effect of shutting her up; she just snorted before returning to scrolling through her phone.

"Farah, that's enough. No need to be bitchy just because you're hungry." Cash met my eyes in the rearview mirror. "Farah gets really angry if she doesn't eat every few hours."

This stick of a girl? Needed to eat every few hours?

Did I mention that Cash's family had impeccable genes? Because – wowza.

"This is Lucky's Tiki Hut," I said, as we pulled up to my personalized spot. Beau had a few spots saved for me, Luna, Miss Elva, and a few of his other favorites. Parking was at a premium here and he wanted to make sure we could always visit him.

Farah cast the restaurant one glance before her eyes landed on the sign designating this as my spot.

"Cute. Um, your own parking spot? Drink much?"

"Never more than two or three. It messes with my psychic powers, after all. And right now they're telling me that you are not a nice person," I said sweetly and swung from the car, not waiting for Cash or Farah to catch up as I stormed into the restaurant. Beau caught sight of me immediately and barreled over.

"What happened? You look ready to gut someone and use their skin for a lampshade," Beau asked, his eyes worried.

"She's a raging bitch. A horrible raging bitch. Be prepared."

"Great," Beau said, pasting a polite smile on his face as the door opened behind me. I moved to the sit at the bar, though I was certain Cash had wanted us to sit at a table so we could all face each other. At least this way, Cash would separate me from she-bitch.

"Beau, always good to see you," I heard Cash say. "And this brat is my sister Farah."

'Brat'? Ha, not even close.

"Pleasure to meet you. I see good looks run in the family," Beau said easily, and I rolled my eyes.

"Oh, stop it," Farah gushed, and I turned my head to see if this was the same woman. "Aren't you just the cutest? I'm so glad to finally meet you."

Had I stepped into a different dimension? Was I in a parallel universe? Or did Farah just dislike me specifically? Beau cast me a curious glance, but beamed at Farah. He led her to the bar – but was smart enough to seat her a stool away from me. Cash quickly took the middle stool.

Farah craned her neck and looked around at the tiki bar.

"Great place. Just the right amount of kitsch, yet an understated elegance. I dig it."

"Farah, do you have something to say to Althea?" Cash asked, drilling a finger into his sister's side and making her jump.

"Yeah, sorry Althea. I'm cranky from lack of sleep and being hungry."

I raised an eyebrow. If that was cranky, then I didn't want to see her full-on angry.

"Sure, no problem," I said politely, but I think we all knew that the terms of our relationship had been set.

"Well, I can certainly help you with the hungry part," Beau said, smiling at Farah as he handed her a menu. He didn't even have to ask me what I wanted to drink – just began mixing a mojito. "Corona?"

"Sure," Cash said with a smile.

I kept my mouth shut – which, if you know anything about me, you know that's virtually impossible. When Beau slid the mojito across the bar to me, I accepted it gratefully and immediately took a sip, letting the cool mint soothe my burning throat.

A part of me wanted to dip into Farah's brain and see if I could read her thoughts – but that violated my code of ethics. And what was the point of having ethics if you ignored them under trying circumstances? Sighing, I swirled the ice around in my drink.

"Burger for you?" Beau asked, and I caught the smirk on Farah's face.

"Actually, I'll have the crab tonight. It's really good here." I turned and smiled at Farah, then looked up at Cash. "Reminds me of the crab we had on our first date – remember?"

"Yes, we need to go back to that place. It was delicious," Cash said, smiling down at me as I warmed underneath his gaze.

"Gag me," Farah said under her breath and I tilted my head at Cash.

"Knock it off Farah or I'm taking you back to the hotel," Cash said dryly, and Farah rolled her eyes.

"Beau, what's good on the menu?" Farah asked.

"Everything. What's your mood?"

"Nothing too…" her gaze slid my way and back, "fatty."

"How about some grilled shrimp skewers with a side of corn on the cob?"

"Sounds perfect." Farah simpered at him.

Beau finished taking Cash's order and disappeared into the kitchen, and my lifeline went with him.

"Are you diving in the morning before work, Thea?" Cash asked, his voice even.

So, the thing is, Cash was technically fine with the fact that I went out diving with Trace on the regular. Because I needed to keep my website updated with new underwater photos for sale, I constantly needed new material. Which meant I was going to keep diving with Trace. But in reality, Cash barely tolerated my time spent with Trace. I have to admit, though, I appreciated that he hadn't tried to outright forbid me from meeting up with Trace. I suspected that even Cash knew I wouldn't tolerate being ordered around.

I don't take to rules well.

"Actually, yes, I'm diving all week. Turns out the expedition I told you about didn't get called off. So I won't be in at work at all."

"Must be nice to just take off work when you feel like it," Farah quipped.

"Yes, it is. That's why I own my own business. I make the rules," I said, smiling brightly at her. Lord, what was up this girl's butt?

"I mean, but it's not really much of a business, is it? Reading tarot cards? Pretty loosey-goosey on the rules there, I'm sure." Farah snorted a laugh.

Oh, so now we were going to attack my profession? Fantastic.

"I invite you to stop by the shop. You'll see that it's actually run with the utmost professionalism. I'm able to close when I choose because I've either worked longer hours to cover my appointments or rescheduled them. And, not that I owe you an explanation, reading tarot has a rich and beautiful history – I help people on a daily basis. With real problems – like their love lives, money situation, job choices, and even planning their families. Not what nail color is the hot trend for this spring," I bit out.

Shit, now I'd stooped to her level and taken a stab at her profession. I held up a hand as she was about to retaliate.

"I'm sorry. I shouldn't have knocked your profession. I believe women should stick together and lift each other up – not tear each other down. I'm not sure what your problem is with me, but you're being incredibly rude and clearly trying to get a reaction out of me. So, I will say this: I make an honest day's work doing something I love, I run a business with my best friend in the world, I have a solid group of friends in this town who I enjoy spending my free time with, and I'm very much interested in your brother. If you have a problem with that – then that's on you. Not me."

Farah measured me for a moment, clearly surprised at how direct I'd been.

"Fair enough," she said.

The rest of the evening followed suit; by the time dinner was over, I was exhausted from trying to pull answers out of a sullen Farah and still make nice with Cash. At this point, I was starting to wish I had driven over by myself.

"I really need to get going. We dive at dawn tomorrow," I said to Cash.

"That's fine. Why don't I run you back home and then I'll come back for Farah?"

"Sounds fine to me. I'll just finish up this fruity concoction Beau whipped up for me," Farah all but sang to Beau, clearly happy that I was leaving. Confusion raced through me – I had expected Cash to tell Farah that he would drop her off at the hotel.

"Enjoy," I said sweetly. "Beau makes the best cocktails." I stood and walked around the side of the bar to lean in and kiss Beau on the cheek. "I hope you poisoned the drink."

I'll give Beau credit – he didn't even blink at my whisper.

"Bye, Farah. It was... interesting meeting you. I hope you have a safe trip back to New York."

I had no idea when she was supposed to go back – but I guarantee you I wasn't going to see her again on this trip.

"Yes, good luck with your little tarot reading shop," Farah said breezily, scrolling through her phone again. A part of me wanted to reach over and pluck the phone from her hand and drop it in the frothy pink drink in front of her.

But I restrained myself.

"Shall we?" I said to Cash, and he nodded.

The silence grew between us during the car ride home until I finally burst out, "What's your problem?"

"My problem? *My* problem?" Cash's voice rose as we neared my house.

"Yeah, your problem. What? Now that your sister is here you're going to act all different around me? It's clear she hates me," I said, my arms crossed over my chest. He hadn't even said anything about my pretty dress, which was completely unlike him.

"Screw my sister – what about the fact that you're going on some expedition you won't tell me about that someone's already been murdered over? Huh? When were you going to tell me more about that? Damn it, Althea!" Cash slammed his fist on the steering wheel and I jumped in my seat. "I've rescued you from two, count 'em, *two*, near-death incidents already. I can't keep doing this! Being with you is entirely maddening."

Whoa boy. That was not what I was expecting. I'd thought we were going to fight about his sister.

"I hadn't realized I was so difficult to be with," I said, honestly shocked at the direction this was taking. Sure, we'd been in some sticky situations together. But I'd thought he was over those.

"It's just... you're not... you don't do anything that's *normal*. And there's magick. And you rush in to save anyone who needs it. And now you're going off on some type of something that you can't tell me about, but Trace knows all about, and I can only suspect that it won't end well. I don't know if I'm cut out for this."

And there it was. The big glaring fear I'd had about Cash all along. Maybe we were just too different.

We sat in silence in front of my house for a moment.

"So I'm going to assume you're not staying here tonight?"

"Are you going to call off the expedition in the morning?"

Ah. So it was an ultimatum then.

"No, I've signed a contract. I have to go."

"Well, then, I suppose call me when it's over. It'll be nice to hear you're safe."

I blinked back the tears that threatened. Somehow we had gone from a fairly normal and happy relationship to – this. And I hadn't seen it coming. It was like hitting a brick wall at sixty miles an hour.

"So what is this then? This is goodbye? Your sister comes down and disapproves of me so that's your excuse to kick me to the curb?" And speeding along behind the tears was my anger.

"It has nothing to do with her."

"Don't lie to me. I'm a freakin' psychic, remember? I can tell when you're bullshitting me. And you are clearly upset that your sister didn't take to me."

"Okay, yes, it would have been nice if you could've

tried to be polite to her."

"Me! I was *nice* to her. In fact, I held back more than I should have. Come on now, Cash, you aren't stupid. Don't tell me you think your sister wasn't being rude."

"Yes, sure, she was being a bit rude. But she's protective of me, is all."

"Oh, so that gives her some license to be a raging bitch? Sorry, I may not have been raised with all the money and prestige your family has – but at least I've learned *manners*." I was surprised to find my hand trembling on the door handle. I looked over at Cash.

Handsome, mouth-watering Cash. Too-good-to-be-true Cash.

"I should've known you wouldn't be able to handle being with a woman like me. Go back to your perfectly perky and boringly respectable corporate girls. I'm sure they'll be perfect for you to parade around on family vacations."

"Now, Thea, that's not fair," Cash began, but I held up my hand.

"This isn't about me getting myself into danger, is it? It's just that you aren't comfortable with the life I lead."

Cash blew out a sigh and ran a hand through his hair.

"It *is* about the danger aspect. I don't want you to be in danger. Shit, I feel like I'm getting an ulcer because I'm constantly worried about you. Is she getting herself into trouble today? What type of magick ritual are they doing now? Is some demon coming to kill her? Will she be kidnapped again? I just… it's too much. I can't even focus through half my meetings. My business is suffering."

My mouth dropped open. This was the first I had heard of any of this.

"Why didn't you say something to me? Why am I just hearing about this now?"

Cash shrugged.

"Because I don't see you changing that aspect of yourself. So what am I supposed to do? I tried to live with it – but I don't know if it's going to be too much."

I took a deep breath.

"Do you want to talk about this some more? Maybe not in the car in front of my house?"

Isn't that always where the most important conversations happen? Sitting in a car in a driveway somewhere? It's never on the couch at home or a nice discussion over dinner.

"I do want to talk about it some more. And I'm not breaking this off, exactly. But maybe we just need to sit with the idea of not dating anymore and see how we feel about it."

There it was. The non-break-up that leads to the break-up.

"Taking a break?"

"Why don't we take a few days. Call me if you need me. Please keep me posted on this expedition of yours. I really don't like the sound of it."

I got out and stood outside his car, holding the door

open for a moment as I held his gaze.

"Funny, because if you were really worried about my safety – breaking things off like this is probably not the way to show it. Seems like a back-handed way to manipulate me into doing what you want."

Cash's mouth dropped open and I slammed the door on his words. I all but ran to my door, and was inside in a matter of seconds. I leaned back against the door and waited for him to knock – to come after me and say we could work through this and become a stronger couple for it.

It was Hank licking my toes that made me realize I'd been standing there crying for several minutes.

"It's just you and me, Hank," I said, crouching down so he could lick my tears. "You and me, buddy."

Chapter Seventeen

I'M NOT GOING to lie and say I flounced off into the night cursing Cash's name and pretending I was a strong independent woman who didn't need no man.

But I did manage to wipe my tears and get up to bed without too many dramatics. After a phone call with Luna where we castigated Cash's manhood, I was feeling mildly better and I lay in bed with my laptop, researching weather patterns for the Florida peninsula.

I mean, I knew trying to sleep was going to be a joke.

So I was surprised when my alarm jolted me awake at five in the morning, all the lights in my room burning brightly, and my laptop tilted on its side on the bed. Hank snored contentedly at my side.

I looked over at the file folder of papers I had printed the night before. I'd spent hours diagramming weather patterns and trade winds, and had a few ideas about what direction we should go in. I would wait to see what Nicola had to offer first, though, before I gave up my ideas.

There's nothing like throwing yourself into a knotty problem, such as a mysterious treasure hunt, to take your mind off of heartbreak, I thought as I jumped in the shower and let the warm water sluice away the grogginess clogging my brain.

And, frankly, I couldn't decide if I was heartbroken over Cash. My heart was certainly bruised, but not broken. We were still in that figuring each other out – testing the waters – phase of the relationship. But, damn, the man was the best thing that had happened to me in a long time. At least in the bedroom.

I sighed and leaned back against the shower wall. I guess we'd just have to see where things stood with us at the end of this expedition. For now, though, I needed to get my butt moving.

I'd told Trace the night before that I was going to meet him at the wharf. I wanted to drop Hank at Miss Elva's, as I didn't feel comfortable leaving him alone while we were on the boat. And frankly, Hank was safest with Miss Elva. There wasn't much that could get past her formidable powers.

"Guess what, Hank? You get to terrorize Rafe all day long," I said as Hank came and licked the water from my leg while I toweled off.

Don't judge. Dogs do weird things like that. So do kids.

I hightailed it through my morning routine, packing my dive bag, shoving my folder of papers in with it, and getting a bag of toys and treats together for Hank. In less than twenty minutes, I was ready to go.

Cup of coffee in hand, I raced out the door.

And stopped in my tracks at the sight of a card tucked under the windshield wiper of my car, the Aztec snake drawing on it clearly visible from my front porch.

"I'm not scared of you!" I said loudly, whipping the card out and crumpling it in my hands. "Come on, Hank."

With that, I floored the car away from the house – and I made sure to drive over the card on the way out.

Nobody had better mess with me today.

Chapter Eighteen

After dropping Hank at Miss Elva's – much to his delight and Rafe's horror – I made my way down to the wharf. Miss Elva had made me promise to stay in contact throughout the day, and I'd tucked my cell phone in its waterproof case in my dive bag, so I'd be sure to remember to text her after each dive.

The early morning light of the sun was just kissing the horizon when I stepped onto the planked floating dock where all the fishing and diving boats were moored. The docks were alive with activity, even at this early hour. Fishermen were packing coolers with bait and checking their lures, while dive boats were securing their tanks. I waved to various regulars – my morning people, as I called them. We all knew each other, and if ever there was an emergency out on the water, you could guarantee that these boats would be among the first to respond.

Trace's boat was tied up at the end of the dock – a pretty red and white boat that catered to smaller, more intimate dive groups. It allowed him to go to some of the less touristy spots, and his services were typically in high demand. I could see that he was already on board, running through his daily checklist and lining up tanks.

"Captain," I called out, smiling at him as I slipped my shoes off and stepped onto the dive boat. Trace immediately took my dive bag from me and tucked it under one of the benches that ran along the side of the boat. The boat was set up with a dive platform at the back that made water entry with a heavy tank on your back easy. The stern of the boat was shaded by a canopy, and a bench ran along each side, with tank slots behind the benches. They allowed you to sit and slide into your BCD vest, so when you hook yourself in and stand up, the tank is attached to your back. It was a nice set-up, and I knew Trace took great pride in his boat. The front had more seating, and a small bathroom was tucked away in the hull below. All in all, it was a solid dive boat without being too large or difficult to handle.

"How are you feeling about today?" Trace asked, stretching his arms above his head. Sunglasses shielded his stunning blue eyes, even though the sun had barely begun to peek over the horizon.

"Not good," I admitted.

"Anything pop for you that we should pay attention to?" Trace asked, easily referencing my psychic abilities without any judgment. Point in Trace's column on that one, I thought bitterly.

"I... well, I've done some studying. I think I may have some idea where to go," I said, moving towards my dive bag. I wanted to show him my maps without Nicola around to see. I didn't trust her and it wasn't my job to provide her with research or direction on this dive. My job was clearly outlined in the contract – take underwater photographs of the expedition. Nowhere did it say anything about assisting in the discovery of the treasure.

I had checked.

"Is that so? What did you find?" Trace asked, his interest piqued.

"Well, I had some help from Miss Elva," I said. "She sent me some info. A photograph of a map. I doubt it's even on record anywhere on the internet."

"Shut up," Trace said, excitement lacing his voice.

"Yeah, I spent almost all night researching it. Not like I was going to sleep anyway." Oops, didn't mean to bring that up.

Trace studied my face.

"You do have dark circles under your eyes. Trouble in paradise? Or just worried about this expedition?"

I debated lying to Trace about my current state of affairs with Cash. But we'd never lied to each other before – and when it came down to it, Trace and I were friends first.

"It looks like Cash and I are taking a bit of a break," I

said carefully, waiting for Trace to crow in delight.

Instead, he reached out and put an arm around my shoulders, pulling me in to him for a squeeze.

"I'm sorry you're hurting."

Well, shit. If he had tried to move in on me, it would have been easy to push him away. But being kind and understanding? Sigh. Now my feelings were even more confused. Maybe I needed a girls' retreat somewhere to cool things down – like a yoga retreat in Arizona.

Not that I did yoga.

"Isn't this cozy. I had no idea you two were an item." A brisk English voice interrupted us.

I pulled away from Trace and looked up to where Nicola stood on the dock. I almost snorted in laughter at the sight of her, but I held it in check. She was dressed as though she were going on safari. A short-sleeved button-down white shirt was tucked into khaki pants that ended at laced-up hiking boots. A wide-brimmed safari hat, reminiscent of Indiana Jones, was perched on her head and her sandy blonde hair was tied in a bun at the nape of her neck. A trim backpack was strapped to her back and she carried a canteen of water in one hand.

"We're not. Are you going camping?" I asked, switching the topic.

Nicola looked down at her outfit and raised an eyebrow at me.

"I have fair skin. I believe this will be sufficient coverage for me, so long as I stay in the shade as well."

"A vampire, eh?" I winked at Trace and he just shook his head, but a smile danced on his lips.

"Not everyone can handle this bright sun. And since I'm not diving, I'd like to protect my skin," Nicola sniffed. She moved to step onto the boat, but Trace held up a hand to stop her.

"Shoes off."

"What? I couldn't possibly take off my shoes," Nicola balked at his order.

"Shoes off or we don't dive. Boat rules." Trace pointed to our bare feet. "Shoes ruin the flooring. That's why they make particular shoes called boat shoes for sailors to wear. The sole doesn't scuff the boat."

Nicola stared at him and two bright pink spots popped out on her cheeks. It was fascinating to watch her control her temper, and I made a note to pay careful attention to this woman. Maybe I'd be able to scan her thoughts at some point and figure out what else was going on behind the scenes of this expedition.

"Well, if that's to be the way of it then," Nicola bit out, forcing a small smile. She handed Trace her pack and canteen and then sat on the dock, taking forever to unlace her boots and fold her socks gently into them. I wondered if she was this precise with everything she did.

Trace held out a hand to help her onto the boat. I was startled to see neon orange nail polish on her feet.

"Cute pedicure," I said, knowing it would throw her off.

"Ah, yes, well. Just a silly affectation really." Nicola waved it away and moved to sit on the bench where her pack was.

"So you aren't diving with us? I thought you'd be going out with us. Also, is it just you? Nobody else from the Institute is joining us?" I couldn't fathom spending as much money as they were on this expedition and only having one person to head it all up.

"I don't dive. And I'll be monitoring and cataloging your finds and impressions as we conduct the dives throughout the day. I'm quite capable of managing a team of two on my own, thank you," Nicola said briskly as she pulled a file folder and laptop from her bag.

"Fair enough. Women are better managers anyway – right, Trace?" I winked at him and he hooted a laugh and shook his head at me.

"Looking to pick a fight this early in the day, are we?" Trace smiled as he fired up the engines.

"Just teasing you," I said brightly, but I was also rethinking my strategy regarding Nicola. Maybe it would be better to align myself with her, as a girls-against-boys type thing – she might let down her guard a little bit.

"Were you?" Trace asked.

"I mean, I do run my own business. Two of them, actually. So I have no doubt in my mind that women are capable managers." I shot a smile at Nicola and she smiled back.

Her first time smiling at me.

I hoped she'd let her defenses down. Because now mine were up even higher.

"So, where are we going today? We still don't have coordinates," Trace said, turning to look at Nicola.

"Yes, well, we weren't prepared to give those coordinates over email or the telephone. We felt it best to wait until contracts had been signed and we were on board the boat."

I looked at Nicola curiously as I moved towards the dock to untie the boat.

"I thought you hadn't been involved in this until your uncle died."

"That's entirely untrue. My uncle was leading the expedition. However, I have been involved since the beginning. He… well, he had entrusted certain documents to me in the event that anything should happen."

Now that statement was reading about a ten on my bullshit meter. I didn't know what she was up to – but I knew she was lying.

Maybe Cash was right about me. Because this is where a normal person would back the heck out and go back to her day job instead of courting danger on the regular.

And yet I found myself untying the boat and standing there calmly as Trace reversed the boat and I jumped back on the bow. As we motored from the channel towards the ocean, Nicola held out a sheet of paper.

"I have a full list of coordinates. I think the best way to proceed is to just start at the top and go through the list."

"Are they rated from, like, most likely to just taking a chance?" Trace asked, reaching for the sheet and plugging the first set of coordinates into his GPS.

"Yes, I believe we are starting with the most likely."

Trace let out a low whistle as location popped up on his screen.

"I hope you don't get seasick – this is at least an hour's ride out."

"It is?" Nicola visibly blanched at the words.

"Didn't you look these coordinates up? They aren't right off the coast. If they were, someone would have discovered the treasure long ago," Trace said easily, his hand on the wheel.

"Ah, no, I can't say that I have. I was a little too wrapped up in my head on the research and not on the actual practicalities of what it would take to get to these points."

I raised an eyebrow at that but made no comment. Settling back onto the bench, I crossed my legs and smiled brightly at Nicola.

"Well, it will give us girls a chance to catch up while we head out there. Oh, and it looks to be a bit choppy today, so I'd hold on." I smiled as Trace bumped our speed up while Nicola grabbed the post behind her, her knuckles going white as she gripped tightly.

Oh yeah. This was going to be interesting.

Chapter Nineteen

By the time we reached the dive site, Nicola was looking pale. Paler? Was it possible for someone as white as she was to become even more pale? But to her credit, she didn't lose it overboard, though there was a time or two when I saw her grimace as the boat bounced across a particularly choppy wave.

"We're approaching the site," Trace said.

I went to stand next to Trace by the wheel to study the equipment. "What's our depth? Will we be able to throw anchor?"

"I'll do a grappling hook. We're at about 120 feet of depth, but side sonar isn't picking up much. I'm not sure we'll see a wreck down here."

"You don't think the wreck is here? Then why even dive?" Nicola piped up from behind us.

I turned to look at her.

"Because shipwrecks don't just sink nicely in one spot. Depending how they went down – if the hull splinters or it hits coral – debris can drift in a wide track from wherever the storm carried it. Just because the sonar isn't registering a full wreck, doesn't mean there isn't something down there. The ocean is vast – it's always worth investigating."

Nicola looked suitably chastised and she nodded, sitting back down and scanning the horizon.

The sun was fully up now, and a light wind kicked up waves just into tiny whitecaps. As dive conditions went, they were as good as could be asked for when you were an hour off shore. I sat down by my BCD and began my safety check, checking my gauges, my O-ring, looking for any deterioration of my regulator hoses. Finding everything suitable, I slipped into my wetsuit, yanking the neoprene up my legs and sliding my arms in the sleeves.

"We're hooked," Trace said from the bow where he'd thrown the line overboard and let it trail until we'd hooked bottom.

"Throw a marker buoy too?"

"Already on it," Trace said, holding up a small orange buoy and tossing it over the side.

"What's a marker buoy?" Nicola asked.

"If the grappling hook causes the boat to drift a bit, we'll be able to see where we were meant to be."

"You mean the boat can drift? While I'm up here alone?"

"It shouldn't. I'll descend on the line and check the

hook before we begin our dive," Trace said soothingly. "But I'll need to go over some safety procedures with you since you're staying on the boat."

I watched as Trace led her through the operation of the radio and the basics of driving the boat. Knowing Trace, we weren't going to venture too far from the boat – I doubted he'd let it out of his sight. He was interested in the treasure – but his boat was his livelihood.

"All set?" Trace asked me.

"Yes, cameras are set. I've checked my gear," I said, turning so he could zip up my suit. Together we did a buddy check on each other's gear, Nicola watching us silently as we did so.

"You're very thorough," Nicola commented when we finished.

"Plan your dive and dive your plan," I said.

"Safety checks are important. You don't want to run into trouble at depth," Trace said seriously.

"So, Nicola, I think what I'll do is just start with an aerial view of the site, so to speak? I'll take wider images as we descend and then as we begin to investigate anything that looks like a man-made reef, I'll take more pictures. Does that work for you?"

"A man-made reef?" Nicola tilted her head in question.

"An artificial reef. Coral will build on structures that end up on the ocean floor. That's why it's often hard to discern what's actually treasure and what isn't – there will be a lot of build-up on it. So it's best to go slow and take our time."

"I have a metal detector as well – though it'll do us little good when we're searching for gemstones," Trace shrugged.

"Why bring it then?" Nicola asked.

"Because it can alert us to the presence of other metal that went down with the ship, so we'll know we're in the right area," Trace said patiently, putting his mask on his forehead.

For someone who was heading up a scuba diving expedition, this woman knew next to nothing about treasure hunting. Trace and I both moved to the dive platform, then, with one look at each other, we each took a giant stride into the water.

There's nothing like descending into the depths of the ocean with a scuba tank strapped to your back. There's all this sunshine and real-world stuff on the surface – then in seconds you are cocooned in a beautiful world of blue water. It's both calming and exciting at the same time.

I held my camera in front of me and documented the dive site from above as we descended. We stayed close to each other, Trace following the line down to the grappling hook. Adjusting my buoyancy slightly, I waited as Trace tugged on the line and made sure the boat was secure.

Flashing me an OK sign, Trace motioned for me to follow him.

It would be a short dive today – you can only stay at

one hundred twenty feet, breathing compressed air, for so long – so I stayed focused.

Where normally I would be bringing my camera up to take shots of the pretty queen angelfish darting by, instead I was firing off shots of any lump of coral that looked odd-shaped.

I kicked along next to Trace, floating comfortably in the water, watching him with his metal detector. In a matter of moments, he raised his hand and gestured me closer. I swam over to him, sinking so that my knees touched the ocean floor.

Trace dug around in the sand a bit – kicking up silt and ruining the visibility for my camera – but in moments, he held something in his hand. He handed it to me.

Initially, it looked like a barnacle-encrusted lump to me. But then I caught the dull gleam of something underneath all the muck. Hooking my camera strap through my arm, I reached down for the dive knife strapped to my calf, while Trace continued to dig in the sand. Using my knife, I began to work some of the barnacles free from the lump in my hand.

And was amazed to reveal what looked to be some sort of a gold cup.

Trace looked at me; I gave him the OK sign and then checked my dive computer. It was time to go up – we couldn't stay at this depth much longer. Pointing to my computer, I gestured to Trace, and he nodded as he pulled out his dive bag. Together we gathered any other 'barnacle-encrusted lumps' we could find and put them in his bag.

As we began our ascent, I couldn't help but feel excitement race through me. We'd found something on our first dive! I wondered what else the ocean floor would reveal to us.

And would it cost us more than we had bargained for?

Chapter Twenty

THREE DIVES LATER, we'd found little else. Nicola'd gone into full-on researcher mode with what we had brought up from the ocean floor, though.

I relaxed back against the bench, my hair pulled into a loose knot on top of my head, a towel wrapped around my bathing suit. Taking a swig from my water bottle, I eyed Nicola as she pulled the cup from a cleaning solution she'd brought with her. With most of the muck removed from the surface, it gleamed dully in the afternoon sunlight.

"This is lovely, just really lovely," Nicola cooed, angling the cup to look for any markings.

"Can you tell if we're in the right century?"

"Yes, yes, it seems to be on par with the year we're looking for. I'm quite certain we're on the right track. Oh, this is just fantastic news. Quetz will be quite pleased."

There was that name again – Quetz.

"Can you tell me more about this investor? You seem to be quite familiar with him," I said, crossing my arms over my chest. Trace was at the front of the boat pulling the grappling hook up. We'd leave the marker buoy in its spot just in case we decided to come back tomorrow.

"No, I can't. Sorry, it's the legalities of it, naturally," Nicola sniffed as she examined the cup with a small eye scope.

"Um, no, actually I don't understand. But then, it's not like I do these expeditions regularly."

"Just imagine it as a large business, and you're just the underlings the commands get filtered down to. You know – you don't really get a say but you must do the work. That's your job."

So much for being friendly with this one, I thought. I opened my mouth to reply but caught a look from Trace. He just shook his head, and I closed my mouth.

Looked like it was my week for dealing with bitchy women, I thought. I crossed my arms over my chest as Trace gunned the engines and we headed for home.

Instead of striking up conversation again, I let the engine noise lull me into a sleepy state of mind as we made the trip back at full speed. I kept flashing through what I knew so far and what I still had questions about. The discovery today had lit Nicola up like a Christmas tree. And even though I knew they were really trying to find El Serpiente, I couldn't help but think they were looking for more. Because – judging from the coordinates on the map

Miss Elva had given me?

We were miles away from where we should have been diving.

Which meant we were looking for an entirely different wreck than the one they were telling us about.

Chapter Twenty-One

I INSISTED ON photographing the entire day's find when we got back to the dock. I laid each piece and shard of treasure out on the gleaming white deck, photographing it all from every angle while Nicola tapped her foot impatiently.

"Really, must we do this? We don't need up-close images of every tiny piece of treasure," Nicola scoffed. I turned and leveled a glare at her.

"I've been hired to photograph the expedition. Part of that means documenting anything found. Don't tell me how to do my job," I said, and she shut up.

Plus I wanted a photographic record of everything we found. According to the contracts, we owned twenty percent of the haul. As far as I was concerned, every last piece was being documented. And I didn't care if it was a piece of broken bottle or the Holy Grail. It was damn well getting recorded.

"All done then?" Nicola asked brightly.

"Yes, go ahead," I said, and Nicola packed the treasures away in her bag – at least taking the time to carefully wrap them first. With a quick wave and a promise to see us at the same time tomorrow, she disappeared down the dock, her hiking boots clomping loudly against the boards. More than one fisherman gave her a curious look.

"So," Trace said, leaning back in the Captain's chair and crossing his arms over his chest as he looked at me. The late afternoon sun warmed his skin to a rosy glow and I couldn't help but smile at him.

"So, that was interesting."

"Did you notice she hasn't mentioned anything about plans for getting her uncle's body home? Or anything to do with the police? She didn't ask us any questions about it. You'd think she'd be more interested in how he was murdered," Trace said.

"I told you there was something off about her."

"What do we do then? Call this off?"

"I'm still not quite certain where we'd come to harm. It's clear they need us. It's after we find the treasure that's the problem."

"You think they'll eliminate loose ends."

"I'm not ruling it out."

There was an uncomfortable silence while we thought about that.

"What happens if we don't find the treasure?"

"I think they'll still try to eliminate us, because we know they were looking for it."

"So this is a catch-22?"

"Maybe. Maybe not. I think we need to call in Miss Elva and Luna, and see what they can do to provide us with protection," I said.

Trace nodded and ran a hand through his hair, turning to look behind him at the dock before looking back at me.

"What were you going to show me this morning before she got here?"

I breathed a sigh of relief. I'd thought for a moment he was going to bring up the Cash situation, or possibly make a move on me. And frankly, I was on emotional overload at the moment.

"Miss Elva followed up with me about finding a map. It honestly looks like a map from back during that time, as well as some actual documentation of weather patterns during that year that the ships were lost. I was going to email it to you, but then I remembered your laptop was stolen. Check it out – I was up all night with this." I pulled the documents out of the file folder and Trace sat down next to me on the bench.

We studied the map together in companionable silence, Trace flipping a page over now and then and making a note or two, then going over my notes. Finally, he looked at me.

"This is not where she's taking us."

I nodded and raised my eyebrows at him in question.

"You think they're following up on different information?"

"I think they're looking for a different wreck," I said.

"Well, shit. If they aren't looking for El Serpiente, what are they really looking for?"

I shrugged.

"I don't know. But I think we need to spend some time researching what else was on that treasure fleet. And if they aren't looking for El Serpiente – then you and I have some diving to do." I held up the map.

"Agreed. So are we going to let on that we know they're looking for a different wreck?"

I turned and looked out at the horizon, where the sun was beginning its fiery descent.

"Not a single word. I suspect they'll kill us if they know."

"We need to find out what else was on those ships."

"Yup. And I think I know just the person to talk to for that."

Chapter Twenty-Two

"CHILD, I WAS starting to worry you didn't get back in safely," Miss Elva called from the porch. Hank immediately ran to the bottom of the stairs and waited, his body wriggling in excitement as I approached the steps of Miss Elva's front porch.

I'd taught Hank long ago that he wasn't allowed to go past the porch steps. Saved me hours of worry about him running out into the street.

Today Miss Elva wore a fairly subdued maroon caftan with white piping along the hem. A single maroon feather was tucked into her bun.

Bending down, I rubbed Hank's ears and scratched his coat before climbing the steps wearily to stand on Miss Elva's porch. The nearly-sleepless night was catching up with me – not to mention the emotional upheaval. All I wanted to do was order a pizza and crash.

"Sorry 'bout that. I stayed after to talk to Trace about our dive plans."

"How'd it go today?" Miss Elva asked, rocking gently in her chair, her pretty brown eyes watching me carefully.

"I can tell you this researcher girl is lying through her teeth. I just don't know what her game is yet."

"Can't catch any of her thoughts?"

"A few, but I haven't dug too deeply. Typically, I don't ever try to read someone's thoughts. But I don't trust Nicola. It's almost like she's blocking me. Almost too good, now that I think about it. I wonder if she practices that around me," I said, leaning back against the railing and crossing my arms. It would make sense – if they had researched who they were hiring for their dive team.

"It's not that hard to put a block up if you know what you're doing," Miss Elva agreed. Hank padded over and pressed his nose into her leg, and she immediately bent down to scratch his ears.

"How'd Hank do today?"

"We had a grand time, though Rafe finally got frustrated and took off. He heard there's a bikini competition down in Key West so he went to check that out," Miss Elva chuckled.

"Of course he did." I shook my head. "Well, let him know I want to talk to him."

"About what now, child?"

"Well, I sat up for a long time last night going over what you sent me. And based on where she took us today?

I'd say they're searching for a different wreck. I'm going to have to research what else was on those ships."

Miss Elva leaned back in her chair and closed her eyes, tapping her finger against her lips as she rocked.

"I'd have to pull my books out for that one, honey. I thought El Serpiente was the biggest treasure still undiscovered – at least from that era and those ships. But... hmm, now that I think about it, I wonder..."

Miss Elva shifted her bulk and got up from her chair, humming as she went into the house, the screen door banging after her. I wasn't sure if we should follow or not, so I just stayed where I was, crouching down to pet Hank.

"Extra treats for you after dinner, buddy," I whispered, and he licked my face in delight.

Miss Elva came back out to the porch cradling a book under her left arm and holding a bottle of beer in her right.

"I didn't get you a beer, seeing as how you look like you're ready to fall asleep on your feet."

"Yeah, it would've just gone to waste," I agreed. I wasn't much of a beer drinker anyway. Too many calories.

This from the girl who was going to go home and order a pizza if there wasn't a frozen one in her freezer.

"Now, I may need to dig a little deeper here, but this might scratch the surface. I feel like I recall something about a sister stone."

My mouth dropped open in surprise.

"What? A sister stone? To El Serpiente?"

"Mmm-hmm, two halves of the whole – one good,

one evil," Miss Elva murmured, sliding reading glasses from a pocket deep in her caftan and putting them on her nose.

I paused for a moment to appreciate the view of Miss Elva wearing reading classes.

"Child, you best stop looking at my glasses like that," Miss Elva ordered, never looking up from the pages she was focused on.

"I wasn't looking at them 'like that.' I like them. They make you look... scholarly."

"And what, pray tell, am I if not scholarly?" Miss Elva looked up and put a hand on her hip.

"You *are* scholarly. You're right. Your house is lined with books. You know way more about everything than anyone in this town. I've just never seen you wear glasses before, is all. It's a good look for you. I promise," I said, holding my hand up.

"Mm-hmm, that's right it's a good look for me. Anything I wear is a good look for me. I make glasses look cool," Miss Elva said.

"You do. I promise you do," I said, wanting to laugh but knowing if I did, I'd be forever banned from front porch chats with Miss Elva.

"Here we go – this is what I'm looking for right here. Or at least it's a spot to get started. The sister stones of Quetzalcoatl. Two halves of a whole, one light and one dark. The Yin and the Yang. El Serpiente and...aha! La Rosa. The rose and the snake, that's right. I'm beginning to remember some of this."

"So the snake represents the bad and the rose is the good?"

"Nope, you've got it twisted. See, most people think snakes are these nasty beasts, but in mythology they were actually considered good. Why do you think the symbol for a doctor is a staff with a snake or two wrapped around it? Snakes aren't bad."

"But how is a rose bad?" I protested.

"Ahh, because a rose lures you in with its beauty, only to draw blood with its thorns when you try to pluck it. Beware the rose. At least a snake warns you before it's going to strike."

There you have it, folks. Logic by Miss Elva.

"So you think they want La Rosa?"

"I think they want both, but they only know where to find La Rosa."

"What would happen if they find both?"

"If those stones fall into the wrong hands? Well, it would be the rise of a whole new empire – all run by someone intoxicated by power, who, it seems, won't hesitate to kill anyone in his way."

"Great, just great. As if this week wasn't crappy enough already – now we have to find *two* stones, or the world is doomed."

Miss Elva eyed me over her reading glasses.

"Child, you need some carbs and some sleep. Getting all cranky up in here like a toddler."

"Fine, I'm going. I'll sleep on this. Email me anything else you find. Or, actually, just text it to me; email is easier to break into. I'm going to go pass out facedown in a pizza now."

"Bye Hankie baby, I'll be smooching on you again tomorrow," Miss Elva cooed to Hank as I waved my goodbye.

Two godstones. Lovely.

Chapter Twenty-Three

I WAS ABLE to sleep this time – although my dreams were plagued with visions of serpents twining around roses.

Frankly, they weren't the worst dreams I've ever had.

I hadn't told Trace about the second godstone, and Miss Elva had yet to find more information – though when I'd dropped Hank off first thing in the morning, she'd assured me she had reached out to an old friend for assistance.

Still no sign of Rafe. Seemed he had decided to hang out in Key West until Hank stopped visiting during the day. I shook my head in disgust as I walked down the dock towards the dive boat. What self-respecting pirate was scared of a cute little dog?

"Ahoy," I said easily, seeing that Nicola was already on the boat. She must have gone shopping after the dive yesterday, because today she was outfitted in a long-sleeved white linen cover-up, though the Indiana Jones hat was still stuck firmly on her head.

"Good morning. Did you sleep well?" Trace asked politely, but winked at me as he held out his hand for my dive gear.

"I slept fine, thanks," I said, slipping my shoes off and stepping onto the boat. "Nicola, good morning. I like your cover-up."

"My cover... oh, my dress? Yes, thank you," Nicola said primly.

"Did you find out anything more about the treasure we found yesterday?" I asked, immediately moving to the bench where my dive gear was set up and beginning my safety check.

"No, but I cataloged it. I'd like to try a new destination today."

"You don't want to explore that area more? I'm surprised. Wouldn't you think that since we found something already, there'd be more to come?" Trace asked, tilting his head in question at her. Today he wore a long-sleeved white t-shirt thrown over some loose board shorts. Something about it made me take a long second look at him today.

Or had I always looked twice at him, but was only just now noticing it?

"No, I don't. I've directions to look in a new area."

Trace raised an eyebrow at me but didn't comment. Instead, he crossed his arms over his chest and changed the subject.

"Did Chief Thomas talk to you about the break-in?"

I shook my head. "No, I haven't heard from him. Why? Did he find anything out?" I was kind of surprised that Trace was bringing this up in front of Nicola.

"What break-in? Do you mean a burglary?" Nicola said immediately, her eyes sharp.

"Yes, both of our homes were broken into recently. In fact, it happened right after your uncle was murdered. Some might wonder if there's a connection," Trace said. We both looked at Nicola expectantly.

"Did they..." Nicola caught herself.

"Did they what?" I asked innocently.

"Um, was there anything unusual about the break-ins?"

"You mean like the Aztec snake painted in blood above your uncle's bed?" I asked sweetly.

"Yes, yes, that's what I am asking." Nicola sighed and tapped her fingers on her thigh. It looked like she was coming to a decision about something. "All right. There's perhaps a bit more going on here than I have let on."

"Gee, ya think?" I asked, rolling my eyes.

"There is a... how do I say it?"

"Another interested party?" I offered, though I'd figured that out already.

"Yes, another interested party," Nicola nodded at me.

"And you didn't think it would be a good idea to warn us about this party?" Trace asked.

Nicola held up her hands – all helpless woman all of a sudden.

"But what could I have said? I can't anticipate their moves."

"It's obvious this person is willing to break the law," I pointed out. "You didn't think it might be a good idea to mention that we're putting ourselves in danger?"

"I would have assumed you could ascertain that yourself, having seen how my uncle was murdered," Nicola shot back.

"Ah, cutthroat, I see. Think for ourselves, defend ourselves, and anticipate danger by ourselves? So we aren't really a team here, are we, Nicola?" I asked, a tight smile stretched across my face.

"I never said we were a team. I was under the impression you understood that. You work for us. We aren't a team. When this expedition is over – and the treasure is found – we part ways. That's it."

And yet it wasn't, and I think we all knew it.

"I think our fee just went up, don't you Trace?" I smiled over at him.

"But!" Nicola's mouth dropped open.

"Yes, I don't recall any information about a known threat to us or our property. Wouldn't failure to disclose something like that fall under your no-bullshit clause, Althea? And now that the bullshit has come to light – so to speak – I think we'll need to negotiate another contract – one that pays at least another fifty grand or so, don't you think?" He looked at me.

I nodded. "At least."

"That's preposterous," Nicola sputtered. "You can't squeeze me for more money."

"You can't knowingly put us in the line of fire and expect us to be happy about it. Sorry, babe. No money, no diving," I said, examining my cuticles, not a concern in the world. In truth, I'd actually be relieved if we could back out of this contract altogether. I wasn't particularly fond of the direction things were headed.

"I'll have to make a call," Nicola snapped, the two bright red spots back on her cheeks.

"Please do so," I said, waving my hand at her carelessly – but inside, my emotions were churning. Maybe we'd get out of this and be in the clear.

Nicola stepped onto the dock and walked away, pacing in the soft light of the early morning sun. She didn't strike me as a bad guy, yet I couldn't help but think she was tangled up in all this nonsense.

Just a researcher, my butt.

"Think they'll give us more money?"

"No way. They'll find another dive crew," I said, relaxing against the bench, my arms stretched across the back, my face towards the rising sun.

"Are we still going out on our own then?"

"Absolutely," I said.

Come on, now – you didn't think I'd actually walk away from that treasure, did you? Someone had to save it from falling into the wrong hands. I'd done some research myself last night, and I had an idea of various museums that we could donate the stones to.

"You'll have the money shortly," Nicola said hotly as she hopped back on the boat, and my head snapped up at her words.

"You've got to be kidding me," I gasped.

I know, not very smooth of me, but honestly – who *were* these people? Was an additional hundred thousand dollars such an insignificant sum to them?

"Yes, your little ploy worked. Unfortunately, we're working against the clock now – first man to the treasure wins."

"Can you enlighten us as to what we're up against?"

Nicola paused for a moment and then turned to look out at the horizon, where the disc of the sun was becoming visible.

"Let's just say this – be happy *we* hired you first."

Chapter Twenty-Four

Another day of diving with no results had Nicola practically spitting nails by the time we got back to the dock.

"Listen, honey, we're doing the best we can. We're staying at depth to the absolute limits of our air time. I'm taking hundreds of pictures for you to comb through. We're trying our hardest. If you want a larger or faster sweep, hire more divers."

Nicola looked like she was going to snap at me, but then she pressed her lips together and nodded once.

"I understand. Thank you for your time. I know you are both excellent divers."

Well, you could have pushed me over with a feather, hearing nice words come from her mouth. Her boss must have lit into her on the phone earlier, as she'd been nothing but pleasant all day.

We didn't get any more information out of her – but

she was pleasant nonetheless.

"Thanks for leading us headlong into mortal danger. At least we're being well-compensated for it," I said, and smiled brightly at her. My inner bitch was dialed way up today.

"Yes, well, let's hope nothing overmuch comes of all this. I'll speak to Quetz this evening. Hopefully we'll be able to drill down to more specific coordinates. It's obvious we're missing something," Nicola said, distress crossing her pretty face for a moment.

"It's a big ocean, lady," I said.

"I'm aware. I'll be back first thing in the morning." Nicola clipped down the dock at a fast pace, already pulling her phone from her pack.

"Well, that was quite the payday," Trace said, looking up from his phone. He held it up in the air for a second. "Just checked my bank, funds were already wired in."

"Someone's got deep pockets," I observed.

"And we're just tiny minnows swimming in a big pond," Trace said.

"I'm really struggling with how Nicola fits into all this," I admitted. "I'm quite certain she's involved – deeply – but I don't know how. I mean, do you think she's capable of killing her own uncle?"

"I think anyone's capable of anything."

It might have been the most honest statement I'd heard in a long time. Because isn't that the truth of it? You think you know someone – then they up and bring their sister to town and suddenly break up with you.

But I digress.

"Soooo, I learned something interesting last night," I said, looking around for a moment and then bending down so the side of the boat concealed my face. Who knew if I was being watched?

"Do tell," Trace said. He came over to sit by me on the bench with his back to the dock, effectively blocking me from view.

"There are two stones. Not one. And once united, whoooo boy. Do we have major powers going on," I said, then filled him on the rest of what Miss Elva had told me.

"Oh, well, sure. Why wouldn't there be two stones? I mean, we might as well add more to our plate. They've only been lost for like four hundred years, but sure, we'll find them both this week. No problem," Trace said dryly.

I laughed at him. "I love you."

Trace pulled off his sunglasses and met my eyes. All of a sudden it became a bit difficult to breathe, as my chest seemed to be tightening under his scrutiny.

"I like those words coming from your mouth," Trace said softly.

"I was just teasing around," I said, feeling awkward and flushed under his gaze.

"Even so. I like them," Trace said again, leaning forward until his lips were hovering just an inch above mine. "Tell me to stop."

"I…" My brain froze. Did I want him to stop? I was

so confused, stressed, and emotionally worn out from this week that I didn't know *what* I thought or wanted.

Trace took that as a yes, and slid his lips over mine in a kiss that seared its way down to my belly. I felt stunned by the power of it – like he was branding me – before I got my wits about me and pulled back, gasping for air.

"Stop," I gasped.

"Oops," Trace said, an easy grin sliding over his face as he put his sunglasses back on – concealing his eyes from me.

"I can't. Let's just get through this expedition. I need to see where I stand with Cash. There's just…it's a lot, okay? Can we just focus on finding these stupid stones? Then maybe we can take an exotic naked vacation somewhere with all our money."

Whoops. Did I say that last part out loud?

Trace's wide smile confirmed that indeed I had.

"Wipe that smile off your face. I'm flustered. You got my hormones going. Just – just let it be for now."

"I'll let it be," Trace said, standing up and stretching. "For now."

I'd be lying if I said a little frisson of excitement didn't work its way through me at his words.

Down, girl, I cautioned myself and breathed deeply. We had much bigger problems at hand.

"I'm going to stop by the store to check in with Luna, stop by Miss Elva's –hopefully she has more info – and then head home to do more research."

"Tomorrow's Friday."

"It is."

"We didn't contract to dive on the weekends – though I suspect they'll push for it. But we'll see. What would you say to some night diving this weekend?"

"You want us to search on our own?"

"I took a look at the map you gave me, as well as the information on the weather patterns. It rings true. I think we should check it out."

"And you think this should be done at night?"

"Two rival groups are hunting for this. When would you suggest we do it?"

"At night, with the running lights off," I sighed. Night diving was one of the absolute coolest – and scariest – things I've ever done.

Predators hunt at night, after all.

"Stay in touch. I'll be on edge until this is over," Trace said, reaching over to squeeze my hand.

"You too," I said.

I mean, what was the big deal? We had two godstones embodying inordinate amounts of power to find before either of two rival parties – perhaps both willing to kill – found them first.

Nope, no big deal at all.

CHAPTER TWENTY-FIVE

THE LUNA ROSE Potions & Tarot shop typically stayed open until six or seven at night. We were flexible on the time – much to the annoyance of uptight mainlanders who wanted hard and fast store hours.

I needed some Luna time. I'd called Miss Elva and she was happy to keep Hank longer for me. I really needed to decompress and catch Luna up on all the drama of this week.

Including that kiss.

Damn that man for getting into my head again. It wasn't fair – he'd never put a move on me before Cash had come into the picture. Now suddenly I had a hot man in my life and Trace was sniffing around like he couldn't get enough of me. It was enough to mess with any girl's mind.

"Luna?" I called, pushing my way into the store. The

lights were still on, but the shop looked empty.

"Yes? Oh, hey," Luna said, popping her head out from the back room. "I'm just changing into a date night outfit."

"Oh, you've got a date? Damn, I wanted to catch up with you," I said, trailing my finger over a table of hand-wrapped soaps.

"Mathias has been working long hours, and he finally had a night free. He scored us some tickets to a show or something in Miami, so I've got to jet," Luna said, coming through the door, tugging the hem of her skirt down.

"Heyooo, check out that hottie," I exclaimed.

She'd paired a black leather pencil skirt with a shimmery sleeveless blouse the color of moonlight. It was demure, yet powerfully sexy at the same time.

"You like? It's a little different for me," Luna admitted, laughing as she did a twirl.

"I do like it. It's like you're letting your naughty side out a bit." I smiled at her.

"Or Mathias is," Luna laughed.

"He's good for you. I'm really happy for you." And I was, I truly was. Luna was my best friend and she deserved all the happiness in the world.

"And here I am being a shitty friend, chattering about my boyfriend while you're in the middle of a breakup," Luna said, instantly contrite. She walked over and folded me into her arms.

"It's okay. Honest, it is. I want you to be happy," I whispered into her shoulder.

"I know you do. But I want you to be happy, too. Should we put a spell on Cash? Something that makes him break out and put on forty pounds?"

I laughed and pulled back from her, using my knuckles to wipe a tear away.

"No. Not yet, at least. Let's just see what this break does for us. Either we'll miss each other enough to work it out, or we'll be done. Then I'll have to deal with Trace."

"Is he still moving in on you?" Luna asked as she picked up her purse.

"He kissed me today."

Luna stopped on her way to the door and swiveled slowly.

"Hold up. Rewind. Explain."

A horn honked from outside, and Luna glanced quickly out the window and back to me. I knew she wanted to hear about Trace, but she was also late for her date.

"Go. Please. You have fun. The gossip will wait."

"This is *juicy* gossip, though."

"I haven't even started on the expedition. Let me just say, when all this is done? You, Miss Elva, Beau, and I are taking a vacation somewhere fancy. My treat."

Luna hooted and shot her fist in the air. "I'm down. I love you. Be safe. Text me. Don't go too long without checking in with someone. Stay behind the wards at your house. Carry a knife."

"Yes, Mom." I laughed at her and waved her off as I headed towards my side of the shop. I wanted to grab a protection amulet my mother had sent me from some exotic country or another. It had been on my mind all day, and I was determined to wear it until this godstone stuff was figured out.

I was rifling around in my drawers when my psychic senses started tingling. Whirling around, I grabbed the closest thing to me – a ritual knife. Holding it tightly in my hand, I held my breath and listened.

"Miss Rose, I'd like to request an appointment."

I shivered at the voice – a staccato rasp of evil.

"I'm not taking appointments this week," I called out. I shifted, trying to see past my privacy screen and into Luna's shop.

Rookie move over here – leaving the door of Luna's shop unlocked. I should have learned by now not to do such stupid shit.

"Oh, but you'll take *my* appointment."

A gun appeared in the doorway.

"By all means. Have a seat."

Chapter Twenty-Six

WHEN WERE PEOPLE going to learn that they'd never get a good reading if I was under duress? I almost shook my head in annoyance.

But something made me realize that this had nothing to do with a reading, and everything to do with the godstones.

Perhaps it was the large Aztec snake tattooed on the throat of the man who stepped through my doorway. Nice placement, if you were into neck tattoos.

My hand clenched around the ritual knife, and he kept the gun trained on me.

"You let go of the knife. I put the gun down. We'll have ourselves a nice talk, eh?" The man's dark brown eyes held mine – and never once did he blink. At easily six feet tall and two hundred pounds or so, he was packing just as much punch as his gun was. His hair was shaved down to just a dark fuzz covering his large head, and he wore a black fitted t-shirt, jeans, and Converse high tops.

Aside from the gun in his hand, he looked like your average everyday tatted-up Mexican-gang type dude. And I was only guessing Mexican by his accent, though there seemed to be a faintly different inflection threading through his words.

I let go of the knife and nodded at the chair in front of me.

"Please, be my guest."

He smiled at me, and in that moment, I recognized his power. They say the most dangerous leaders are always the most charismatic. With one flash of his blindingly white teeth, he'd shown a charm that I'm sure had sent more than a few women flocking to him.

Some woman just can't resist the bad boys.

"Nice tattoo. Thanks for spray painting it on my fence. You must have thought I needed some help decorating," I said, deciding to go on the offense.

"I'm sorry if we got off to a bad start." He flashed his charming smile again. "I hope I didn't ruin your fence."

"Oh, it's not ruined. I painted over it the same day. Like you were never even there," I said, taunting him a bit. When I saw the spark in his eye, I knew I'd found one of his weaknesses.

Ego.

This man wanted to be idolized.

"Maybe we can start again. My name is Tlaloc."

One word. Apparently he thought I would have heard of him, because he was watching me closely, as if he expected to see some kind of reaction.

"Hmm, like Tupac?"

Annoyance flashed in his eyes again. I was getting good at this game. Hopefully not so good that I wound up getting shot.

"Something like that. It is a great and powerful Aztec name. The name of a warrior. A sorcerer. A god."

"Gee whiz, that's a lot of job descriptions you got going on there," I said, picking up and shuffling my tarot cards. "Is that what you've come to see me for? Advice on your career path? I'd go with being a god if I were you. You'll be able to get away with sooo much more than normal people."

Tlaloc slammed the hand holding the gun down on the table, making my crystal ball fall off its holder and go rolling. I lunged forward and caught it with one hand – conscious that the gun followed my every move.

"So disrespectful for someone who is but a mere mortal."

"Is that what you're trying to tell me, then – that you're a god? You want me to bow down?"

Tlaloc's gaze skimmed my chest before returning to meet my eyes. The charming smile was back.

"I wouldn't mind seeing you on your knees."

Ew.

"Tlaloc, why don't you cut the bullshit and tell me

what you want?"

Tlaloc eased back in the chair, resting one foot on his knee. I stared at his Converse sneakers. Do gods wear Converse? He might want to up his style game if he wanted to convince people he really was a god.

"I'm just here to chat. Among friends, you see," Tlaloc said.

"Friendly is holding a gun to my face?"

"I didn't shoot it, did I?"

Apparently that's how a god showed he was your friend. By not shooting you in the face. I wondered how many people he'd convinced of his godhood, and just what level of crazy I was dealing with here.

"Thanks," I said dryly. "Seems like you couldn't show the Professor the same courtesy."

"The professor was a loose end. I don't like loose ends. He tried to work with too many sides – get what I'm saying?"

"So killing him was the answer?"

Tlaloc shrugged and looked around.

"Nice shop," Tlaloc commented, the subject closed. I looked over at Herman and the panda, sitting on the leopard-print chair.

"Yes, I like it," I agreed with him.

"You've been diving a lot lately," Tlaloc continued, raising an eyebrow at me.

"Aside from this business, I also run an underwater photography website. It's one of my passions," I said primly.

"Taking lots of photographs this week?"

"Always," I said with a smile and he smiled back at me.

We were all just friends here, right?

"Find anything…interesting to photograph this week?"

"Oh, you mean El Serpiente? No, I didn't."

His eyes widened at my words, and he jumped from his chair to leap across the table and grab my throat in one large hand. I screeched, then clawed at his hand as he began to squeeze tighter, cutting off my air.

"Do. Not. Say. That. Name."

I nodded as best I could with his hand clutched around my throat. He squeezed once more, making me squeak in protest, before easing his hand away from my throat. He stood over me, and looked down at me with a kind smile on his face.

"You'll do well to remember that I am the true ruler. Those stones are from my bloodline and are meant to return to their rightful owner. Nobody speaks their names but me."

"That's fine. But could you calm down with all the attacking me? I don't know anything about these stones, so there's no way I could have known not to say their names out loud," I said, trying to act huffy, but in all reality trying to keep him from seeing how much he had shaken me.

"Fair enough, Hermosa." Tlaloc ran his hand down

my face and I shivered. He stepped back, but didn't sit. Instead he paced my small shop, his gun in hand.

"How much?"

"Excuse me?"

"How much money do I have to offer you for the stones?"

"I don't have the stones, Tlaloc." At least that I could answer honestly.

"I'll triple what they are offering you." I could read from his energy that he was being dead serious.

"That's going to come in at close to half a mil, then," I said, raising an eyebrow at him.

"Done." He smiled at me, then reached into his pocket and pulled out a card. He tossed it on the table, and I picked it up. On one side was the same Aztec snake I'd seen too many times already. On the other was a phone number.

"You've got a business card?"

"Don't be cute. That number is for you alone. I switch my other phones daily."

"Ah." There really wasn't much more to say to that.

"You'll call, if you find them, or are close."

Now here's the thing – when someone is holding a gun on you, you'll pretty much say anything to get them to leave you alone. Right?

"I'm sorry – I don't really understand the significance of these stones. I'm certain there are more valuable treasures to be found," I said, then wanted to smack myself in the forehead. I could've just said yes, and the evil crazy gun-wielding man would have left my shop. But noooo, I just couldn't keep my mouth shut.

"You really know nothing of the stones? Did the people you work for tell you nothing?"

"I'm not entirely sure who I'm working for. And, no. It's all on a need-to-know basis. They gave me the names of the stones," I lied, then paused as his lips tightened. "And that was it. I had to Google what I could on the rest," I finished.

"Ah, Wikipedia. I love it, but sometimes it is not so accurate, eh?" Tlaloc pursed his lips and shook his head at me before sitting down once again.

Shit. Now he was cozying up for a chat. I really needed to learn how to keep quiet.

"This tarot you do – it's like a power, yes? You can divine things?" Tlaloc asked with a small smile.

"I suppose you could call it that. Though I don't always 'divine' so much as lead people in the right direction."

"Ah, but ages ago you might have been considered a great seer of fortunes. This power, well, it passes down through the blood, yes?"

I shrugged one shoulder, noncommittal. I wasn't about to bring my mother into this.

"I am a descendant of the great Yaolt, a man who reigned supreme over the Aztec empire and was touched by Quetzalcoatl himself."

"Is that so?" I smiled, all friendly-like. I didn't need more bruises on my throat.

"It is indeed, Hermosa. Yaolt reigned for years, bringing great fortune as well as doling out punishments when needed. Everything he touched turned to gold – and his word was law. It has been revealed to me, through our family, that the fall of Yaolt began when these precious stones were stolen from him by the Spanish, to be transported to the Spanish royal family. Of course, it was only natural for their ships to go down. Those stones were destined for my family – my race. Not for the Spaniards. The power they hold? It can change the world."

"And you're the man to do it? Change the world, that is?"

"Yes, Hermosa. Do you know the amount of good I could bring to my people? Great fortunes, bountiful harvests, health and strength – ah, yes, the Aztec people would rise once again, claiming the land and the power that is rightfully ours."

"What about the 'doling out punishments' part of it?"

"Ah – with every good comes the bad. Like two sides of a coin, yes? You need only flip it."

"*Ahora.*" A voice spoke from inside the shop – it was only just then that I realized Tlaloc was not alone. Of course he wasn't. These types of men traveled well-guarded.

"I must be off. We have a deal, yes?"

I looked down the cold steel barrel of the gun held

inches from my face and said the only thing I could.

"Yes, of course we do."

Chapter Twenty-Seven

I DIDN'T PEE my pants or anything.

But I did sit there for a minute or two after he left, my body visibly shaking as I forced myself to calm down.

Tlaloc was a bad dude. Understatement of the year and all, I know.

Once all my limbs had started working again, I hightailed it from the shop. Still shaking, I pulled out my phone as I drove away, and called Trace.

"Yo," he said. I'd put the phone on speaker.

"I… I…" I didn't really know what to say.

"You changed your mind about that kiss?"

"Aztec gang guy just held a gun to my head."

"Holy shit, damn it, Althea, where are you?"

Like this was my fault?

"On my way to Miss Elva's."

"I'm on my way."

I'd gathered my wits about me by the time I pulled up to Miss Elva's, but Trace was already pacing the porch. Seeing him made me want to go all girly and run to him – so instead I straightened my back and shot my nose in the air.

I'm a contradictory one.

"Thank god," Trace said, coming down the steps to wrap me in his arms.

"You all right there, honey?" Miss Elva called from the porch, and I pulled away from Trace to sit down on the top step and wrap my arms around a visibly agitated Hank.

"Hey sweetie, I'm fine. Mama loves you," I said automatically as Hank slathered my face in kisses.

"What the hell happened?" Trace demanded.

Hank glanced at Trace and then back to me.

"Hey, stop with the angry voice. Hank doesn't like fighting."

"Sorry, Hank," Trace said, bending down to scratch Hank's ears.

"I'd stopped at the shop to talk to Luna, but she was leaving for a date. Stupidly, I didn't lock up behind me while I went to grab an amulet my mom sent me."

"That's a nice amulet right there. Good energy." Miss Elva nodded at the amulet where it now hung around my neck.

"Thank you. And, well, yeah, he walked in and held a gun on me," I said, mechanically going over the details. By the time I was finished, Trace was kneeling in front of me to check my throat.

"You're already bruising," he swore.

"I'll be fine. I grabbed some of Luna's magickal healing salve. I'll be healed up by morning."

"I can take those bruises away for you, child," Miss Elva said, her eyes on mine.

"No, I think they need to stay for a bit. Remind me not to be so damn stupid."

"I think we need to dive tomorrow night. On the map sites Miss Elva gave us." Trace leaned back against the porch column and crossed his arms. His hair was pulled back from his face, and I could see a twitch in his jaw.

"I'm down. I say we find these stones before either of these other two groups do."

"Did Luna teach you the stasis spell?" Miss Elva asked.

"No time."

"Looks like you're staying for dinner. You'll be making time."

You don't say no to Miss Elva.

Chapter Twenty-Eight

Hours later I had calmed myself down, learned a stasis spell – something that I never thought that I would have to learn – and was snuggled comfortably on Miss Elva's sofa. She'd served up an excellent shrimp gumbo for dinner and I was beginning to slide my way into a semi-conscious state.

"Miss Elva?" I almost mumbled, then pulled myself up into a sitting position before I fell asleep.

"Yes, child?"

"How come I can't just use that locator spell to find the treasure and call it a day?"

Miss Elva stretched out her legs and examined her neon pink pedicure.

"You could certainly try. But it works better when you have an emotional connection to the item you're looking for – or when there are highly charged emotions surrounding the need to find or be found," Miss Elva shrugged.

"I have a lot of emotions about finding these stones. Mainly the emotion of not wanting to die," I said, annoyed with this whole expedition.

The bruising on my neck hadn't been given much chance to bloom – between Miss Elva's insistence on healing them and Luna's salve, my throat was pretty much back to normal.

Everything was normal. Except the parts about someone who believed he was a god tracking my every move, and Nicola withholding information about who she worked for.

Maybe Cash was right. Maybe it was time to try and walk the straight and narrow. I was a psychic, for Christ's sake – I should know better than to get myself involved in these situations.

"Learning lessons, girlie, learning lessons," Miss Elva said, shooting me a look. Hank was snoring lightly on her couch, his stomach facing up and his paws moving ever so slightly. I wondered if he chased a squirrel in his dreams.

"Learning to trust my instincts? Learning to not get involved in stupid shit?"

"Maybe. Or maybe it has nothing to do with that, and instead it's learning that you're always going to walk a different path than most, that your true nature is to be a risk-taker."

Look at Miss Elva – laying some truth-bombs on me tonight.

"I mean, I suppose that I know that, in some respects. Running my own business is a risk," I shrugged.

"Yes, but it's still considered respectable. Even if what you sell is slightly off the beaten path. I'm saying embrace what you are. Your magick, your psychic abilities, your need to help others – that's all a part of you. Don't shrink from it or try to fit yourself into a mold. People like you and me, child – we have no mold. Own it."

I felt kind of like I was in the locker room before a big game and the coach was giving me that winning speech that would send me onto the field, ready for battle. And in some respects, that's what it was. Except this wasn't sports, and the battle was for my life.

And for the godstones.

I couldn't forget those stones. But at this point, I only wanted to walk away with my life – oh, and, you know, save the world from the godstones' falling into the wrong hands.

The usual.

"Okay, I got it. I'm a warrior."

"There you go, child. 'Bout damn time you realized it. Now if I was you, I'd be letting that Cash know exactly what I thought of myself, and that he can either sign up for that ride or step aside for a more deserving dude. I don't know what happened between you two this week, but you'd better knock that simpering, moping stuff to the side. You've got bigger things to worry about. And the last thing you need is some man telling you to tone it down."

"You are, as always, a hundred percent unequivocally right, Miss Elva. I don't want to tone it down. In the slightest."

It felt good to say those words – to own that fact. I felt a lightness settle in my gut – as if I were claiming my own power. And maybe, in a way, I was. The world doesn't ever tell you that you're okay just the way you are. From makeup commercials to 'proper' jobs to what your body should look like – we're constantly bombarded with all the ways we're supposed to change ourselves, the subliminal message being that we aren't good enough the way we are.

And damn did it feel good to stop and say, wait a minute – this is me.

Take it or leave it.

Chapter Twenty-Nine

I SLEPT LIKE a baby that night – although I don't get that saying. Don't babies wake up like every hour and cry? Either way, I was refreshed and ready to tackle the day. I know – it's perverse, isn't it? You'd think being held at gunpoint would bring me nightmares for weeks. But Miss Elva's pep talk had really resonated with me.

"I'm a warrior, Hank. Like Xena, except I'm no princess." I chuckled and got out of bed; Hank's ears had popped up at my laugh.

I suppose he was happy to see me in a good mood, not moody and sad like I'd been all week. Dogs are very tuned in to our emotions – and I had no doubt he'd been trying extra hard this week to comfort me.

"You're the sweetest, most cutest, most loveable, bestest dog I've ever met," I cooed to Hank, and he wiggled on his back to the edge of the bed so I could scratch his tummy as he convulsed in delight.

There's nothing like a dog to lift you up when you feel blue.

I worked my way through my morning routine at a fairly quick pace, and congratulated myself for only thinking about Cash once during that time. I'm not a cold-hearted witch, you know. I'd just been a little distracted since our argument and he wasn't the only upsetting thing I had to dwell on this week.

It's amazing how we can compartmentalize things when we need to.

As I walked down the dock after dropping Hank off at Miss Elva's, I thought about my feelings for Cash, for Trace, for my life in Tequila Key. I could change it all if I wanted to – tell Cash I would change, stop reading tarot, even move to another state. But then I wouldn't be true to who I was as a person. Instead, I would have to learn to deal with my feelings like a big girl – and continue on the path I'd set for myself.

Which, at the moment, included finding some damn godstones without getting offed in the process.

Trace was already at the boat, though just a thin line of light could be seen on the horizon.

"Do you think today's the day?" he asked as I slid my sandals off and handed him my dive gear.

"I feel like today's going to be significant, one way or the other."

"Did you get a good night's sleep? I was worried about

you after I left Miss Elva's."

"Surprisingly, I did. Miss Elva gave me a pretty good pep talk. It made a difference – I think. In any event, I slept well."

"Good, because tonight, you and I are diving solo. I want to check out a spot or two – I think I've finally narrowed it down. At least based on the maps Miss Elva gave you."

"Lovely. Night dives are always so… interesting." I winked at him as I stepped on board and moved to the bench to check my BCD over.

"Since when are you scared of being a shark snack?" Trace asked.

"I'm not. I'm more concerned about who else might be out on the water."

"You think they're diving at night?"

"So far we haven't seen any other dive teams leave from here – at least none we don't recognize. Unless they're coming around from the far side of the island."

"I'm not too worried about it. My boat's fast, and we know these waters."

"Okay then. I'll see you at sundown."

"What's occurring at sundown?" Nicola asked from the dock and I jumped. I hadn't heard her come clomping up. I turned to see that she had picked up a pair of flip-flops. It seemed she was finally getting the hang of things – though the safari hat was still jammed on her head. Someone really needed to introduce her to straw hats.

"Dinner," I said, reaching up to grab her pack, then helping her onto the boat. I was surprised she let me take the pack – I really wanted to take a peek at whatever was tucked away inside.

"Ah, so you two *are* an item then." Nicola nodded as though confirming the suspicions she'd had all week.

"No we aren't. We're friends. Eating dinner. With other friends."

"If you say so," Nicola shrugged, clearly not believing me. Whatever; I was a warrior, I reminded myself. I didn't need to explain myself to anyone.

"Where are we diving today? Should we go back to the first site where we actually found treasure?" I asked, changing the subject.

"I think we've zeroed in on where we want to be today. It's somewhat near the first one, but a few miles further up the current."

"Makes sense." Trace nodded and held out his hand for the coordinates. He plugged them into the computer, then his eyes met mine briefly before he went back to looking at the screen.

"Looks to be about a thirty-minute ride. Not too bad," Trace said easily, but I caught the note in his voice.

"Where are we today?" I asked lightly, crossing to peer over his shoulder at the screen.

Shit. It was damn close to where Miss Elva had showed us. How had they found the dive site?

"Sure, I've been in that area. It should be easy to dive," I said, pasting a smile on my face and turning around to look at Nicola.

"Good, let's get going then. I'm hoping today is the day," Nicola said briskly, sitting down and crossing her legs. I noticed she wore one of those seasick bands on her wrist and I wondered just how difficult it had been for her to be rocking on a boat all week if she suffered from seasickness.

The money must really be worth it.

The ride out to the site was fairly choppy and I saw Nicola bite her lip more than once as the boat hit a high wave. She was going to have a tough time on the surface today. That's the nice thing about diving – once you're under the water, the surface waves mean nothing.

Trace dropped a grappling hook when we got close to the coordinates, and in short order we were hooked up and our gear was on our backs. As we made our way to the back of the boat, I glanced back at Nicola as the boat bobbed in the waves.

"Apply pressure at your wrist. You can also use a pressure point under your knee. Google it on your phone. It'll help."

Nicola nodded her thanks at me.

"I've got some medicine in the bathroom too. Feel free to use it," Trace added.

"Thank you both. Please... be safe," Nicola said, and I glanced at Trace. This was the nicest she'd been to us all week. Maybe getting seasick was making her lose her edge.

THREE TEQUILAS

In moments we'd reached the floor, and I waited while Trace checked to make sure the grappling hook was secure. Our depth was only eighty feet today, which would allow us more time to explore. Looking around, I could already see that we'd need the time.

Trace glanced at me and flashed me an OK sign and I nodded, pointing immediately to what I had seen. He glanced over and then back at me, his eyes wide in his mask.

A broken mast lay across a swath of coral, its wood concealed by algae and various forms of muck – but I was still able to discern the unnatural shape of it. We immediately swam to where the mast lay and I began to take pictures, making sure to document the area, as I followed Trace and his metal detector.

Trace held up his hand for me to wait and I kicked around in circles as he investigated something on the floor. Patiently waiting, I examined the coral head in front of me, reaching out to wave my fingers at a fairy basslet that had popped his head out to investigate me.

And froze when I realized that the glint of green sitting on the ledge of the coral was not, in fact, a fish – but a stone.

A shiny, rough cut, emerald, to be exact.

My heart skipped a beat and I almost held my breath before reminding myself to –duh –not hold my breath with a regulator on. Picking the emerald up, I turned it in my palm. An almost rectangular shape, it was cut in rough angles and gleamed dully – a deep, rich green. It wasn't big enough to be the godstone, but it filled almost my entire palm.

Which meant we were awfully damn close.

Turning, I tugged on Trace's fin and he glanced back at me. I laughed into my regulator as his eyes went huge behind his mask.

We'd done it. We'd found treasure. Maybe not the prize we were looking for, but as far as I was concerned, this was still part of our haul.

And it was stunning.

Trace grabbed my hand and did a little dance under the water. I handed him the emerald and watched as he held it up, turning it over so that it caught the light. On impulse, I picked up my camera and shot his picture. In moments, Trace had handed the emerald back to me and was already beginning to scour the rest of the ocean floor with the little time we had left at that depth. I saw him shoot his hand in the air as he uncovered something else. Turning, he held out his hand.

Another emerald.

It was happening – this was really happening. We'd found treasure – most likely *the* treasure. I tried to contain myself, but a squeal of excitement still escaped me as we began our ascent.

With a total of eleven emeralds tucked in our bags.

Chapter Thirty

I SQUEALED AS soon as we broke the surface and Trace laughed at me. We rocked in the waves, kicking towards the boat, laughing in excitement. I grabbed the ladder and pulled myself up with Trace following close behind.

Nicola was curled on the floor, her hands wrapped around her knees. She dragged her face off her knees and looked at us dully.

"Please tell me your smiles mean you found something."

"Oh, I don't know, do a bunch of big freakin' emeralds count?" I asked, pulling one out of my carry bag. The emerald caught the light and gleamed, its green color mirroring the hue of sea water over a sandy floor.

Nicola's mouth dropped open and she jumped up, but then steadied herself with a hand on the pole as the boat dipped with the waves. Centering herself, she waved me over.

"That's... wow, that's stunning," Nicola said, awe lacing her voice. She grimaced as another wave crashed into the boat and I looked around for the first time.

"Ah, Trace, I think we've got some weather coming up here," I said, pointing to the dark clouds hovering ominously on the horizon. The waves had now turned into full-on whitecaps, and I could tell that Nicola wasn't going to make it through these swells.

"Why don't we go back in and see how the weather turns out this afternoon? Usually these storms blow over fairly quickly," I said, gently pushing Nicola to sit back down on the bench.

I was surprised when she nodded her agreement. I'd figured they'd be so hell-bent on finding El Serpiente that she would insist we push through, now that we'd found actual treasure. Another wave smashed the boat and I glanced over at Trace.

"Trace? Want to call it?"

"Yes. These waves are getting nasty. Let's get in before we end up like the wreck we're trying to find."

Nicola closed her eyes at his words and leaned back, wrapping both arms around the pole that held the canopy up. Nodding at Trace to go, I secured our equipment. At the last second, I snagged a marker buoy and dropped it – just in case.

"Let's go."

Trace hit the throttle and the boat raced towards

shore, slamming into the high waves, the storm at our back. I braced myself and kept an eye on Nicola, worried she was going to let go and go bouncing overboard. Turning, I looked back, and could just make out the small orange dot of my marker buoy flailing in the swells.

We should have checked the weather before this dive. Though, now that I thought about it, I was certain I'd checked it on my phone this morning, and nothing had registered other than sunny skies.

Or had the curse of El Serpiente reached us – and was just now rearing its ugly head?

Chapter Thirty-One

Once we were docked, Nicola seemed to perk up considerably. The ginger ale Trace handed her probably helped as well.

I had laid the eleven emeralds out on deck of the boat and was racing against the storm to take pictures of them all. They looked stunning, the depth of their color all the more striking against the white of the deck.

"Okay, you've got enough images," Nicola said, reaching over and grabbing one of the emeralds.

"I'll say when I'm done," I said, hip-checking her and making her stumble back.

"Althea," Trace warned from behind me, but I didn't look up, just continued to click away.

Silence fell, the only noise coming from the wind and rumbles of thunder behind me, and the occasional shout from fishermen docking their boats.

"Althea," Trace said again – sharply this time. I looked up from my camera to find myself facing my second gun in less than twenty-four hours.

"You've taken enough photos," Nicola said softly, and I stepped back, my camera in my hands.

"By all means, take the emeralds. All yours, darling," I said softly, my eyes on hers. Nicola stepped forward, but then realized she'd have to drop the gun in order to gather the emeralds.

"Step back, both of you. On the benches."

I went and sat on the bench next to Trace.

"Take the emeralds, Nicola; I don't really care. Do you, Trace?"

"Not in the slightest," Trace said easily, leaning back and looping his arm over my shoulders. I leaned into him as the storm raged out at sea, coming closer by the minute.

Nicola put the gun down and hurriedly shoved the emeralds into her pack, taking care to constantly scan the dock as well as keeping an eye on us. When they were all packed away, she came to stand before us.

"We won't be needing your services anymore. Thank you for your time. I'm sorry I had to pull my gun on you," Nicola said.

I did a quick scan of her energy to see if she was being sincere. She was.

"We didn't find El Serpiente, though," Trace said.

"I'm telling you that your services are no longer needed. And I must insist you stay away from that dive site.

Unless you want to die."

I jerked my head around to meet Trace's eyes. What was this woman playing at?

"But our contract says we only get paid if we find El Serpiente."

"Yes, and the contract also states we can terminate as needed. It's terminated. Althea, please hand over the SD card to your camera."

"I don't think so, sweetie. I own the copyright to those images."

Nicola sighed, clearly annoyed with me, and reached for her gun, tucked in her waistband.

"Fine, fine. I don't really care. Take the pictures, take your damn emeralds. It doesn't matter to me. Good luck making it out of here alive yourself," I said angrily as I pulled the SD card from my camera and handed it to her.

Nicola stopped as she was about to step off the boat.

"Are you threatening me?"

"No, I'm not threatening you! I don't want your stupid stones. I'm telling you that *I've* been threatened, and the 'other interested party' is not messing around. Watch yourself."

Lord knows why I was even telling her to take care of herself, after she'd just pulled a gun on me, but my read of her was still unclear, and there was something inside me saying I needed to warn her. Frankly, it was no skin off my back. At this point, we were all playing for our own lives.

"Who threatened you? Why didn't you inform me?"

I looked at Nicola incredulously. "Why would I tell you? I have no idea what team you're on."

"I'm on the team that's trying to keep everyone alive," Nicola bit out.

She was telling the truth, too. I wished I could read her thoughts, but her mind-blocking game was excellent.

"His name is Tlaloc. You can't miss him. Big snake tattoo on his neck? He's after the same stones you are. He's offered us triple your rates. Maybe I'll go tell him what we found today."

I said the last part as an empty threat, but the very real fear that flashed across Nicola's face surprised me.

"If you tell him, you're signing your own death warrants."

And with that she was gone, racing through the first drops of rain as they began to fall with the big fat plops that signaled an impending cloudburst.

I opened my mouth to speak to Trace, but in that instant the sky opened up, drowning my words as we ducked for cover under the canopy. We held on as the winds raged against the boat.

I stared out at the black horizon, and wondered just what game we were really playing here.

Chapter Thirty-Two

"I HONESTLY CAN'T believe we're going back out. We're crazy. We must be crazy," I said to Trace later that night as we motored away from the dock in the darkness.

"Oh, we're for sure crazy. As crazy as you are for giving her the wrong SD card."

Yeah, about that. I'd decided early in the week that I couldn't trust Nicola, so I'd been switching SD cards throughout the week. The one I'd given her only held the pictures from the ocean floor – I still retained the one where I'd photographed the actual emeralds.

"We signed a contract," I pointed out.

"Somehow I feel like people who'll hold you at gunpoint aren't going to care much about contracts."

"Fine, maybe not. But I've got all this downloaded and on file with Miss Elva. If anything happens to us, Chief Thomas will have evidence."

Even as I said the words, I realized how crazy they sounded.

Trace sighed as we motored quietly into the dark water, his eyes scanning for any other running lights. There was only a slip of a moon tonight, so we were cruising in near-total darkness.

"And yet, here we are," Trace murmured.

"Here we are," I agreed.

We sat in companionable silence for a while, me thinking about why Trace and I got along so well, and Trace – well, who knew what the hell Trace was thinking about.

"Talk to Cash at all?"

Ah. Well, there you go.

"He texted me today to check in on me. I told him I was fine," I admitted. That had been the extent of our communication, but it had been enough to put a little crack in the armor I'd put around my heart.

Damn it, I missed him.

But at the same time, I didn't miss him at all. I loved diving with Trace and it had been a fun – if somewhat insane – week of being able to dive all day long. Even if it was for nefarious purposes, diving was always fun in my book.

"That guy," Trace said, shaking his head. I nudged him with my shoulder.

"Shut it," I said.

"Pretty cool finding those emeralds today, huh?" Trace asked, changing the subject.

"Yeah, I couldn't believe it! I was just waiting on you, looking at this little fairy basslet, and then boom! I realized the green I was seeing wasn't actually from the reef."

"I can see where the excitement comes in. Man, what a rush," Trace said, running his fingers over his chin.

"Think we'll find something tonight?"

"I think we'd better be prepared for anything," Trace admitted. He reached up and flicked his running lights off, plunging us into darkness. The only glow came from his GPS screen, and he pressed the button to dim that to the lowest level as well. In seconds we were traveling in virtual blackness.

"Want to go up on the bow and keep your eyes peeled?"

"Yeah, that would probably be best. Jeez, I had no idea how weird it is out here with no lights at all," I murmured, feeling my way forward until I found the edge of the boat. Following it to the front, I laid down on the deck so that my head was at the front of the boat and began scanning the water.

Pro tip here – when you're on the water with no lights on, bring your head close to the water level. Not only will your eyes adjust to the light and be able to see anything that disrupts the water – but you'll be better able to hear the water slapping against the hull of a boat in front of you.

Assuming that boat also had their lights off. Otherwise, Trace would be able to see the boat far before we reached it. And wasn't it just ironic that I was pulling some James Bond stuff this evening?

I stayed quiet as we motored along, my eyes constantly scanning, until Trace whispered to me.

"Almost there. You can come back."

It had taken us longer than it normally would to get to the dive site, as Trace had kept his engines on low. I didn't mind, though – it was actually quite beautiful once my eyes had adjusted to the darkness. And the water had calmed down after the storm that had blown through earlier.

I tried not to let anxiety about what we were preparing to do get into my head. I mean, any normal person might think going out on a dive in the dead of night – with nobody minding the boat above and in the middle of some high-stakes treasure hunt – might not be the smartest thing in the world to do.

But far be it from me to point out the obvious.

Trace had checked all our gear and set it up prior to leaving the dock, so all we had to do was slip our wetsuits on and click into our BCD vests. In a matter of moments we stood at the back of the boat.

"Remember. No light until the bottom."

If I clicked my dive light on at the surface, any boat in the area would immediately see us. But if I waited until we were at the bottom, they'd need to be right over us to see that we were down there. I'm not saying it decreased our risks by much, but it helped. Marginally.

"Got it," I said and we held hands as we leapt from

the back of the boat.

Now, let me tell you something. There is nothing that really prepares you for an eighty-foot descent in pure darkness. You keep blinking as your eyes scramble to find any source of light – anything at all.

Instead it's like sinking into a void. The only light was the glow coming from Trace's dive computer. His lit up – mine didn't. I didn't do enough night dives to justify the expense of a fancier computer. As we neared the bottom, Trace clicked on his light, immediately illuminating the world around us. I blinked for a moment at the shock, the brightness hurting my eyes, but quickly clicked my light on as well.

We stayed close together, kicking our way along until we came to kneel in the sand, and took a moment to allow ourselves to adjust. Night diving is a whole different beast. Your vision is limited to the scope of your light – and even as strong as they make dive lights, it isn't much. In other words, a predator – such as a curious shark – may literally be dancing just outside the beam of your light, and you would have no clue about it.

I shivered for a moment, then shook my head. The likelihood of me getting picked off by a shark after the week I'd had was slim, so I focused on the task at hand.

We began our scan, staying neck and neck, sweeping the beams of our lights back and forth as we carefully catalogued the reef and the ocean floor before us. And, boy, was the reef teeming with activity. I wished I'd brought my camera with me, because the entire reef was out feasting. All the cool stuff that stayed tucked away and hidden during the day came out to feed at night.

Trace and I froze at the exact same instant. Call it diver's instinct. Call it experience. But we both heard the sound of a boat engine at the same time.

Without hesitating, we began our ascent.

I tried to breathe easily as we stopped at fifteen feet for our safety stop. We hadn't been down on the floor for very long, so we wouldn't have to decompress for as long. But there was still no way we'd shoot right to the top. Trace reached over and looped his arm through mine; then, reaching down, he clicked off my flashlight.

Together we floated in the water, holding onto each other, as the noise of the engine drew closer.

I almost choked when Trace jerked me up, pushing me towards the ladder. I rushed from the water, ducking low as I scurried to the bench, and moved so that my tank slid into its slot. Keeping my head down, I unclipped my BCD and slid out of it, dropping to my knees on the deck of the boat. I crawled across the floor and put my hand on the key. I waited as Trace climbed the ladder and moved quickly to get his tank off as well. In seconds, he was by my side.

"Stay down," he whispered, putting his hand over mine and turning the key to start the engines.

Now, you can be as quiet as you want, but sound travels over water. The rumble of an engine starting up is unmistakable.

As is the sound of gunfire.

"Go!" I hissed, and Trace floored the throttle.

I toppled back, catching my arms around the rung of the captain's chair, and held on for dear life, burying my face into the deck.

Shots kept firing and I wanted to scream, but couldn't bring myself to do anything other than hold on and pray to the goddess to put a bubble of protection around us. Trace held the steering wheel in one hand, his head barely peeking over the top to see, as we roared across the water at full speed.

Neither of us said a word until we'd drawn close to shore. Trace flicked on his running lights and decided to mix in with some of the other boats taking a nighttime cruise around the water. Obviously he wanted us to intermingle with the other boats for a while before docking, in case we were being tracked.

"Did you see anything?" Trace finally asked, looking down at where I crouched on the floor.

"Not a damn thing," I admitted.

"That was insane."

"I'm just glad you and I reacted the same way," I admitted.

"As soon as I heard that hum of the engine," Trace said, and motioned shooting upwards with his hand.

"Yup, I thought the same thing. Get out now."

"That was scary as hell. I'll be having nightmares for

weeks," Trace admitted as he finally brought the boat into dock. I wouldn't admit it to him, but my entire body was trembling with those little shakes you get from adrenalin surges.

"It was like those ghost stories around the campfire – you know the ones, where they hold the flashlight up, but suddenly it goes dark?"

"Totally," Trace agreed, as he docked the boat and I jumped out to tie it up. I wasn't worried about being back on the dock; there was enough activity that I highly doubted anyone would take a shot at us here. "I'm happy to keep you company at night if you want help keeping the nightmares away."

"Very funny," I said as I hopped back on the boat to stuff my gear into my dive bag. Trace and I both worked with more speed than usual – we wanted to be off this boat.

"I'm coming with you to Miss Elva's," Trace said as we walked quickly down the dock and toward his Jeep.

"Yup. I've got an idea what's going on here – and I know just the person we need to be talking to."

"Good. Because this shit can't keep happening. I don't think my poor heart can take it."

I shot Trace a glance as we got in the Jeep.

"Right, like your heart can't take a shock?"

"My heart can't take not being with you."

It was said with a combination of snark and seriousness, so I wasn't sure what to think. I slanted a look at him.

Trace pursed his lips at me. "Baby."

Okay, he was teasing then. The moment passed as I laughed and settled into the front seat of the Jeep.

We had bigger things to worry about than our hearts.

Chapter Thirty-Three

"So you think Miss Elva isn't telling you something?"

"I think *Rafe* isn't telling me something," I said, without thinking.

"Rafe?"

"Um, Miss Elva's pirate ghost."

Trace didn't comment, so I assumed he was taking it in stride. After all, with what we'd just been through, not much was going to faze him. I couldn't remember if we'd ever specifically discussed Rafe in front of him, but I wasn't going to worry about that detail right now. Trace would just have to deal with it, one way or the other.

Miss Elva didn't look to be on her front porch, but the living room windows blazed with light. Her house looked homey and inviting, a beacon of warmth and safety on a dark day. I kind of wanted to curl up on her couch and never leave.

We clambered up the porch steps and knocked on the door.

"Well, child, what happened? You're back sooner than I expected," Miss Elva said, raising an eyebrow as she looked at us through the screen door. Hank danced around behind her, delirious at seeing me.

"We were shot at. Put a damper on the dive."

"That'll do it," Miss Elva agreed, pushing the screen door open and ushering us inside. I immediately plopped onto her deep Restoration Hardware couch – yes, Miss Elva shops at Restoration Hardware – and snuggled in with Hank. He licked my face – out of concern, I liked to think.

Who was I kidding? Hank kissed everyone hello.

"Is Rafe back from Key West?" I asked as Miss Elva swung into the living room from the kitchen carrying three bottles of Corona. Passing them off to us, she settled in her armchair and took a deep pull. Tonight Miss Elva was wearing orange and turquoise paisley wide leg linen pants and a loose turquoise linen top. I wondered if this was what Miss Elva considered loungewear. It was a far cry from my I Heart NY sweatshirt and old sweats that I put on to watch a movie at home.

"Rafe! Come down here," Miss Elva called, and Rafe poofed into view behind her immediately.

"Yes, my lovemountain?" Rafe cooed.

"Althea wanted to talk to you," Miss Elva said, pointing at the couch where I was cuddled with Hank.

Rafe sniffed when he saw Hank, and crossed his arms over his chest. His hat wobbled on his head, but I'd yet to see it fall off. I wondered if you got to choose the outfit you wore when you came back as a ghost, or if you were stuck with whatever you'd been wearing when you died.

"I hope you're taking that devil beast home with you," Rafe said. Hank tilted his head at him, looking cute as could be.

"Rafe, he's harmless. You've got to get over your fear of the dog," I said, and Trace looked at me.

"Is he here? And he's scared of Hank?" Trace snorted.

"I will slit your throat in your sleep, you miscreant!" Rafe shouted, flying in front of Trace.

"Cool it with the insults," I told the ghost, then turned to Trace. "Rafe wants to murder you in your sleep now."

"Interesting. I did feel like a… change in energy or something. It got colder in front of me, that's for sure," Trace said, his eyes wide as he looked around – and through – Rafe.

"I'll make you feel cold forever," Rafe promised.

"Tone it down, Rafe. I have some questions for you," I said, patting a spot on the low table in front of me. "Come, have a seat. I promise to keep a hold on Hank."

Rafe sat, but kept a careful eye on Hank.

"We've been diving for some shipwrecks this week. Looking for a particular treasure," I said.

Rafe immediately looked interested.

"Treasure's my favorite."

"I know it is. You happen to hear of a treasure called El Serpiente? Or La Rosa?"

Rafe immediately looked away and up at the ceiling.

"What are you looking at, Rafe?"

Rafe just whistled and examined something on the far wall.

"Rafe," Miss Elva barked, and Rafe jumped. He turned back to me, chagrin on his face.

"I may have heard of those," he conceded.

"Would you happen to know where the ships are that contain those treasures?" I asked carefully, running my hand down Hank's side.

"I might," Rafe said, and I threw my head back and stared at the ceiling as I counted to ten.

"Rafe, you knew they were looking for that treasure all week. Why didn't you just tell me?" Miss Elva scolded, and Rafe flew to her side.

"I was mad that she kept dropping that stupid devil beast off at our house," Rafe said, wringing his hands as he hovered over Miss Elva.

"Rafe – the sooner we find the treasure, the quicker Hank gets to go home."

Hank perked up at his name, rolling over to expose his belly and stretch his legs in the air. Rafe was unswayed by this display of cuteness; instead he crossed his arms once more and sniffed.

"I was not aware of that," he finally admitted.

"What's going on?" Trace asked. I'd forgotten that he

couldn't hear Rafe's side of the conversation.

"Basically, the pirate knows about the treasure and withheld information on purpose because he was mad that I kept dropping Hank off here," I summarized.

"You're making me sound like a spiteful woman," Rafe sniffed.

"Well, if the shoe fits…"

"That's it! I'm not helping you. Find the treasure on your own. It should remain in the water anyway. Nasty business," Rafe said, zooming into the kitchen. It still gave me a moment's pause to see him zip through a wall.

"Rafe. Back in here this instant," Miss Elva said in her I-mean-business voice. Even Hank rolled over and sat up, and Trace straightened a little in his seat.

You don't mess with Miss Elva when she uses that voice.

"Fine, but I'm only here because you are the sweetest, most voluptuous beauty of a woman I've ever seen," Rafe said, his words dripping with adoration for Miss Elva.

"You tell Althea what you know about that shipwreck. She's getting shot at and hunted down – bad people want this treasure. It's better if we get it and protect it, keep it from getting into the wrong hands."

Rafe visibly gulped at her words.

"I didn't know that. I'm sorry, Althea," Rafe said earnestly and I nodded at him. "That's bad news. Those stones… I don't know. I was once blinded with lust for them. They'll do that, you know. But time has shown me what a mistake it was to go after them," Rafe hung his head.

"You searched for these treasures?"

"I went after the treasure fleet. It wasn't just a hurricane that sank those ships. I had a hand in taking some of them down. And I had the treasure! Ever so briefly, that is. Until the storm came."

My mouth dropped open and I gaped at him.

"Are you telling me you attacked the treasure fleet and plundered the treasure?"

"Yes, I am."

"And then your boat was shipwrecked after you obtained the godstones?"

"Yes, nearly twenty-four hours later. Ahhh, but for those twenty-four hours!" Rafe brought his hands to his lips in a kissing motion. "It was bliss. The stones – they blind you. All I could see was the joy, the honors the royal family would bestow upon me when I brought the stones to them, and how it would elevate my position in society. It was – well, it was the best day of my life."

We were all silent for a moment as we devoured that information. It was enlightening and terribly sad all at the same time.

"What's happening?" Trace whispered to me, and I started.

"Oh! Uh, Rafe was a pirate at the same time the treasure fleet sailed. He went after and intercepted the godstones. He was telling us how wonderful the stones made him feel – as though he would finally be accepted back into society and that the royal family would shower gifts upon him."

"Oh," Trace said, taking that in. "That's sad."

"I never made it home," Rafe said.

"What happened, Rafe?"

"I… I don't know. We could sense the storm coming. There's tells on the sea, you know. We were discussing turning our boats back. We'd made the decision to head back to land and postpone the journey. But, then we just… didn't." Rafe shook his head and held up his hand to forestall me from speaking. "I will warn you against these stones, Althea. They make you… not right. It's like they blind you with their love or something. I don't know. I just felt that I was cocooned in this glow of power, that nothing and no one could beat me. I was the Almighty, you understand? And so I ignored my first mate and turned the boat around. The storm arrived shortly thereafter and decimated the boat."

Rafe didn't have to go into more detail. I could imagine the horror of a storm ripping through your boat at sea.

"When I drowned… I can't speak of it."

I took a deep breath. What do you say to someone as they relive the last moments of their life?

"That's… I don't know what to say Rafe," I finally said, helplessly.

"It's done. I made the choice – blinded by greed. I paid the ultimate price."

There was a moment of silence as we gave Rafe a little space to come back from the raw emotion of his story. He was sitting on the arm of Miss Elva's chair, and she murmured something to him that seemed to perk him right up. Then I said, "There's no record of your ship being near the treasure fleet, though."

"Of course not. Pirates didn't record their passages. Do I need to explain the definition of pirate to you, woman? We operated on the principle of stealth," Rafe said, back to his old self. I shook my head at him.

"I understand. But some pirates still kept ship's logs."

"Not me. That's what made me the best at what I did. Until those stones."

"You wouldn't happen to remember where you were when the ship went down, would you?"

I held my breath at that question – turning to raise my eyebrow at Trace in a hopeful look.

"Of course I do."

I almost dropped my beer.

"Rafe!" Miss Elva admonished. "Why didn't you tell me?"

"Nobody asked."

Chapter Thirty-Four

And that is how Trace found himself on a dive boat the following day with a white witch, a voodoo priestess, a pirate ghost, and a psychic.

"This is certainly the most diverse crowd I've had on this boat," Trace decided as we motored out onto the water.

It was one of those perfect days – just a light brush of wind to tease up the waves. The sun shone in an almost cloudless sky and a gull swooped lazily over the boat as we cruised in the direction Rafe indicated. We weren't going by coordinates this time. Instead we were just taking a cruise to see if Rafe really could remember where his ship had gone down.

And if we did find his boat, it would be an undiscovered wreck in the Keys. I shook my head as I thought about the legalities. We'd have to file an admiralty claim.

"This way," Rafe pointed, and I repeated his instructions to Trace.

"This here's a nice boat," Miss Elva said, looking around at the boat. She wore a screamingly bright pink bikini covered by a cream crochet cover-up. Did I mention that Miss Elva owned her curves? I needed to borrow some of her self-confidence on occasion. Luna looked flawless as usual in a demure white bandeau swimsuit that somehow looked elegant and sexy at the same time. A wide-brimmed straw hat with a polka dot ribbon and large Jackie-O sunglasses completed her look. I felt woefully underdressed in my raggedy diving suit and oversized t-shirt. I didn't care, through – I felt excitement hum through me as we followed Rafe's directions to his hidden spot.

"Over here. Of course," I murmured as Rafe guided us several miles past where Miss Elva's map had indicated. It made sense, based on the timeline of events he had outlined for us.

"What's the depth here?" I leaned over Trace's shoulder to check. I hooted with laughter when I saw. "Sixty feet? Shut up. That's awesome."

"I'm trying not to freak out," Trace admitted. That depth would lengthen our dive time and allow us more time to explore.

"This feels right," Rafe said, relatively subdued himself.

"Cut the engine," I said softly. Trace did, and I moved

to the front of the boat and threw the anchor instead of the grappling hook today.

Rafe flew out of the boat, hovering just above the water. His face dropped for a moment as he looked down, then he nodded.

"Here," he said, pointing down.

I indicated the spot for Trace and he noted it.

"Rafe, are you okay? We don't have to dive here if you don't want us to," I said, crossing my arms across my chest as I looked up at the ghost floating above me.

"It's done. I have had several hundred years to come to terms with it all," Rafe shrugged.

"And now we've got each other, baby," Miss Elva said softly, and Rafe went to sit by her. She murmured something in his ear and he nodded, looking out over the water.

"I'll keep an eye on stuff up here," Luna said. I was glad she had come with us. We'd been able to catch up on some of our much-needed gossip time this morning. I was feeling marginally better about the Cash situation, though I suppose being shot at puts anything into perspective.

"Thanks," I said.

"Now you remember that stasis spell I taught you, child. Do your best to hold it before you bring those stones up."

"I will," I said, though I was tremendously glad Luna and Miss Elva were both on the boat to take matters into their own hands once we retrieved the stones.

"Let's do this," Trace said and we geared up.

"Back in a bit," I called before jumping into the water. My adrenalin was cruising at a fairly good clip, and I was almost trembling with excitement as we descended to the floor.

I saw the ship immediately –half of it, at least. I wondered where the other half had drifted to. The stern of the ship lay on its side, tucked between two long strips of reef, all but hidden from above. I could see how probably hundreds of boats had zipped over this site, thinking it was just another lump of coral.

Trace and I swam to the stern and I marveled at the ship. For some reason, this wreck hit me fairly hard. I knew someone – well, the ghost of someone – who had once lived and died on this ship. Granted, he hadn't practiced the most noble of livelihoods, but there was still something incredibly sad at seeing a ship, once destined for great travels and adventure, torn to pieces on the ocean floor. I blinked back the tears that threatened.

Running my hand over the Captain's wheel, I imagined Rafe standing here long ago, wind in his hair. It made me smile to think of him in all his glory. I glanced up to see Trace motioning me from the spot where the deck splintered off. He wanted us to go into the hull. Nodding, I kicked over and swung myself under the side of the ship, taking a moment to allow my eyes to adjust to the dim interior.

Rays of light filtered into the hull from small portholes along the side of the ship, but the rest lay in darkness. I clicked on my dive light to assist, and was startled to find that the silt covered...

Pretty much nothing.

The hull was empty except for a single box that Trace was now hovering over. How could that be, I wondered? Had the cargo been strewn for miles through the storm? Or had this wreck already been ransacked? I looked around for signs of any recent disturbances, but for all intents and purposes the wreck looked completely untouched.

Trace hefted the crate between his hands and looked at me and shrugged. I gave a thumbs-up signal and he nodded. We might as well take a look at what was in this crate; then, if nothing else, we could do a couple more dives throughout the day to scour the deck and surrounding area.

And trust me when I say I knew that, once this was all over, I'd be back to look for anything else Rafe had tucked away on his ship.

I kept my eyes on the crate in Trace's arms as he began to kick around in circles at our safety stop. A sudden wave of evil hit me so hard I almost choked as my stomach roiled in disgust. I met Trace's eyes behind his mask to find them glassy – like the lights were on but nobody was home. Yet when he focused on me with a decidedly evil squint to his eyes, I realized that someone was definitely home.

It just wasn't Trace.

My mind scrambled as I stayed at fifteen feet of depth, counting down the time until I could reach the surface. If Trace didn't drown me first. He'd kicked closer and was reaching out to me with one hand, his other hand hooked through a handle on the crate.

I dodged his reaching hand, smacking him as best I could against the weight of the water. Forcing myself to breathe, I began the stasis spell Miss Elva had insisted I learn.

"I call upon earth, air, fire, and sea, let all maintain harmony, as I will so mote it be."

Now, let me tell you, it was damn hard to try to speak a spell into a regulator, while maintaining my safety stop *and* avoiding an attack by the godstone that had taken over Trace. But I remembered what Luna had instructed me about intent. So, pouring my everything into the words, I repeated them over and over as Trace came at me again.

His hand closed around my regulator hose just as my spell seemed to work. There was brilliant flash of white light, then Trace was holding my shoulder, his eyes wide behind his mask as we floated in the water. Reaching out, I took the other handle of the crate and pointed toward the surface.

With two kicks, Trace and I broke the surface, the crate between us.

I spit my regulator out at the ladder.

"Luna! Miss Elva! It's in here. I barely put a spell on it!" The words rushed out as Luna was already pulling the crate to her. I stared at the brown streak the crate left across her white suit.

So she *could* get dirty.

"What happened there? It was like I blacked out or something," Trace said. We were both still in the water, holding onto opposite sides of the ladder as the boat dipped gently in the waves.

"The godstone took over. You came after me. I'm quite sure you were trying to drown me."

Trace's mouth dropped open and he shoved the hair back from his face, his mask around his neck.

"Althea... I would never, you must know that."

I reached out to touch his shoulder.

"Hey, I know. It's okay. Magick is a powerful thing. I'm just glad I managed the spell in time. Remind me not to try doing magick underwater again. It's tough trying to talk into a regulator."

"I just... I..." Trace was visibly ruffled by the experience.

"Let's get out of the water and see what we found," I said gently, climbing the ladder ahead of him and moving across the boat to sit on the bench and tuck my tank into a holder.

Luna, Miss Elva, and Rafe all crouched around the crate. Miss Elva looked up at me.

"Nice work on the spell."

"It took over Trace for a moment. Things got a little dicey. We're good now." I gave a shout as I was picked up suddenly. Trace whirled around with me in his arms before lowering his head to my forehead.

"I'm sorry. It scares me to think what might have happened."

"Nothing happened," I said, squirming in his arms. I wasn't the lightest load to carry, and I wanted him to put me down.

"Still," Trace said.

"Put me down. It's fine. We're fine."

Trace complied, but first he let me slide down his torso so all my bits touched his.

I'd be lying if I said I didn't enjoy it.

I gave him a flirtatious look, then turned to the crate, knowing that my face was flushed.

Rafe hovered over the crate, reaching out one hand to almost touch it but then pulling back.

"I packed this crate. This very crate. See the stamp in the corner? That is my mark," Rafe said, indicating a small stain on the wood that looked like a trident.

"It's a lovely mark, Rafe," Luna said gently and Rafe nodded, not saying anything else.

"Luna, we've got to do an extra level of protection here. I'm not feeling good about this," Miss Elva said, and Luna nodded. Together they stood, holding hands over the crate. I appreciated that they hadn't tried to pull me into the circle. It was one thing to teach me magick, but another thing entirely to throw me into advanced-level spells when we were dealing with a godstone.

Stepping back, I leaned against Trace as we watched Luna and Miss Elva raise their arms to the sky, calling upon the goddesses for assistance in securing the contents of the crate. More flashes of light ensued and Rafe fluttered behind us, doing his best to stay out of the way of the magick. I didn't blame him, either, as he'd been pulled through the veil on one prior such occasion. I didn't think he wanted to go back. He was having too much fun here with Miss Elva.

"We should be good," Miss Elva said as they closed the circle and stepped back.

"Screwdriver?" Trace asked, offering one to Luna. She grabbed it and knelt by the crate. I was still tripping out over the smear of silt across her pristine white suit, but decided to let it rest as she made quick work of the cover of the crate.

We let out a collective breath as we peered inside.

"The necklace!" Rafe said, ecstatic at the sight of the necklace lying on the top layer of the crate. It looked like it had once been wrapped in cloth that had deteriorated through the years. It was what I would call a statement necklace – huge chunks of emeralds set in gold cascaded down to a large emerald pendant.

"Is this the godstone?" I asked, pointing at the pendant.

"No. It was going to be a gift to my queen, but now I shall gift it to my new queen." Rafe bowed and, momentarily forgetting that he was a ghost, bent to lift the necklace from the crate. I blinked back another wash of tears when he faltered, realizing he wouldn't be able to pick it up, and put his hands behind his back.

"Here, Rafe, I'll get it for you." I jumped in and picked up the stunning necklace; making a great show of it, I curtsied in front of Miss Elva. "A queenly gift for a queen."

"It's positively stunning. Rafe, thank you," Miss Elva said. She inclined her head – every inch the regal queen – as I slipped it around her neck and clasped it in the back. It made her crochet cover-up look like a million bucks – though I imagined the necklace was worth far more than that.

"My lovemountain, it looks beautiful on you. A treasure for my treasure. Do you like it?" Rafe asked, wringing his hands as he fluttered around Miss Elva.

"It's the best gift anyone's ever given me, Rafe. I'll wear it proudly," Miss Elva said, and Rafe crowed in his delight.

"Uh, guys, I think we have a problem," Luna said. She had removed the layer of wood the necklace had rested on, and I gasped at what was underneath.

A singular emerald, as large as an ostrich egg, lay nestled in what appeared to be remnants of cloth and straw. I could make out something etched into its side, but had to bend closer to see what it was.

"La Rosa," Luna and I said together.

The evil godstone. It was beautiful to the point of sheer decadence. It seemed to absorb even the light of the sun, making the stone almost appear to glow from within. A rose had been painstakingly etched in one side and I could see a shallow groove chiseled into another side.

"Is the groove where it fits with El Serpiente?" I asked, pointing at the groove but not daring to touch the stone.

"Yes, it fits there," Rafe said, staring down at the stone. "I separated them for travel. Even I could sense their power when they were together. Now I wonder if separating them is what doomed me."

"Rafe, only half of your ship was down there. And no other crates. Do you think you can tell us where the other half of your ship lies?" I asked, watching as Luna covered the godstone with the wood again. I was glad she did – it was making me almost itchy to look at it. Even contained by a spell, the power the stone gave off was unmistakable.

"I think we'd better get this stone in to Miss Elva's house. I'm not liking the vibe it's giving off. We need more power to hold it," Luna said, casting a worried look at Miss Elva.

"I agree. Rafe, tell them where you think the rest of the ship is. We need to get that other stone before anyone else does."

Rafe darted off the bow of the boat and began to zip at high speed over the water, scanning close to the surface, until he dove into the water. I gasped.

"What happened?" Trace leaned in and asked me.

"Rafe just dove under the water. I don't know why,

but I had just assumed ghosts couldn't swim. Which makes absolutely no sense now that I say it out loud."

"Here," Rafe called from about a football field's length away.

Trace pulled up the anchor as I started the engine. I piloted the boat to where Rafe hovered over the water and Trace dropped a marker buoy where Miss Elva indicated.

"Mark the coordinates too, Althea," Trace called back.

"Already on it," I said, saving the coordinates on the boat's computer.

"Ready to head back to shore, Rafe?" Miss Elva asked, standing at the bow of the boat and watching as Rafe looked sadly down into the water. The boat fell into silence as we gave Rafe a moment to collect himself. Trace shot me a questioning glance, but I just shook my head for him to be quiet.

Finally Rafe looked up and moved to Miss Elva's side.

"I've said my goodbyes. I'm ready now."

I made a note to try and find something to bring back for Rafe – anything, just so he had something of his own to add to Miss Elva's house.

Though the necklace wasn't a bad haul itself, I thought as the sun caught the stones wrapped around Miss Elva's neck.

Not bad at all.

Chapter Thirty-Five

"You know, night dives haven't exactly been favorable for us," I pointed out to Trace as we headed out, yet again, to dive for the stones.

It had been an intense afternoon. La Rosa was a feisty stone and it had taken many spells, some old, *old*, magick, and a call to one of Miss Elva's Cuban colleagues before the stone stopped trying to take control of whomever was closest to it.

I'm not even going to talk about the brief moment it had tried to possess Hank.

I'm telling you – you think you know all the weird there is to know in this world, and something else pops up to surprise you.

Though I probably had a slightly higher dose of weird in my life than most.

"You bring along any magick bag of tricks in case we

actually find this other godstone?" Trace asked from next to me. I leaned on the Captain's chair with him, craving closeness after the week we'd been through. Aside from the occasional blare of a boat horn, the night was quiet. We cruised along at a relaxed speed, hoping not to encounter any other boats on our way.

I wasn't too worried about it – we were far from any of the coordinates that Nicola had given us. It was unlikely that we'd encounter any other boats out where Rafe had led us.

"I left a message with Chief Thomas today. I asked him to keep an eye on Nicola. I don't trust her. She claims she's staying in town, but we'll see."

"Why would she call off the diving right when we were close to discovering more?"

I'd had some time to think about that and figured I had the answer.

"I think she's filing an admiralty claim."

"Shit, of course," Trace breathed.

An admiralty claim would legally allow Nicola to take anything from the wreck we'd discovered. It would also go a long way towards getting her investor to continue to funnel money into the dive. Recoveries of that level can prove to be long and costly. It would make perfect sense for her to get the legalities straightened out before proceeding.

"You'd think – with the deep pockets they have – that they would've had an intern stationed outside the courthouse. Ready to race inside and file the claim," I joked as we drew closer to the dive site.

We were operating the same as last night – no running lights and moving quietly. The wind had kicked up a bit and the only other sound to reach us was the slapping of waves against the side of the boat.

"Or paid off some judge to handle it," Trace observed as he turned the engines off. "Drop anchor."

I'd already moved to the front of the boat. The splash of the anchor hitting the water sent shivers down my spine. I thought of what Miss Elva had slid to me before we'd left her house.

"Put this in your BCD. Dive with it."

Her tone had brooked no disagreement. I'd done as she'd told me, and now I wondered what she'd seen that I hadn't. Why was it that my psychic sight was strong for everyone but myself? You'd think I wouldn't get myself into so damn many situations.

It didn't take long for us to get geared up. Trace and I moved silently next to each other by the light of nothing but the moon. As we stepped to the back of the boat, our tanks on, divelights in hand, I turned to look at Trace.

"Am I crazy? Like certifiably undateably crazy?"

"Oh, you for sure are," Trace's teeth flashed white in the darkness. "But you're my kind of crazy."

He jumped in the water and I followed on instinct, smiling around my regulator. Damn him for making me feel all warm and tingly inside.

The feeling didn't linger long as we descended in darkness again, our arms hooked through each other's, the only glow coming from the small screen of Trace's dive computer. Instead, the razor edge of adrenalin sliced through me, putting me on high alert.

Trace clicked on his flashlight, sending a blinding shock of white through the dark water. I fumbled for the switch of my own light, adding my beam to his as we hit the floor.

We took a moment to orient ourselves, but it only took seconds for me to locate the battered remains of the bow of the ship. As my flashlight swept across the wreck, the beam of light landed on the figurehead – a proud eagle – sticking straight up from the bow of the boat. I tugged Trace's arm and we swam over together. The figurehead wasn't very large for a boat this size, and I wondered if I could get it off somehow to bring back to Rafe.

Trace tugged my arm and I shook my head. You'd think I wouldn't be getting so distracted by going shopping for Rafe right now. I rolled my eyes at myself. We had bigger things to focus on.

I didn't even need to swim over the ripped hole in the deck to feel the pulse of power emanating from inside the ship. I grabbed Trace's arm and turned him to face me. Holding the flashlight under my face so he could see me, I indicated that I was going in first – and that I knew for sure the stone was inside.

It was somewhat surreal, dipping into the dark hull

with only the beam of my flashlight slicing through the water to light my way towards one of the most powerful items I'd ever heard of. Several crates lay in this hull, and more were broken and on their sides. Though I itched to explore them all, I knew which one the stone was in. It all but glowed in the water, and the power radiating from the box was almost palpable. I swam to it and instantly realized that we had a problem.

This crate was long and much larger – the size of a trunk, really. And it was securely chained to the wall of the hull.

Trace swam next to me, recognizing the problem as well. Pulling out his dive knife, he began to pry the lid off the crate. Reaching out, I put my hand on his arm and stopped him.

We couldn't be stupid about this – not after what the last stone had managed to do.

I ran through the spell – with some enhancements suggested by Miss Elva – three times before I felt the pulse of power ease back. Even so, it felt different to me. I couldn't quite explain it, but I felt safe to proceed. Nodding at Trace, I held the light on the chest as he pried it open.

We had to wait a moment for the silt, dislodged when he had opened the crate, to settle, but I could already make out a world of treasures in the crate. Gold doubloons were piled on top of each other, mixed with rough-cut emeralds. An intricate gold cross, chock full of emeralds, lay on top of the loot. I snagged it and tucked it into my BCD. I wouldn't be able to bring Rafe the figurehead, but this would at least be something for him.

I gasped into my regulator at what had been revealed when I removed the cross. Beneath it lay the godstone. The symbolism of it resting beneath a cross wasn't lost on me, and I reverently picked up the stone and held it in the beam of light from Trace's flashlight.

It was stunning – as La Rosa was – but in a different way. Similar in size and rough cut, it held the same ethereal glow. And the Aztec snake etched in the side was the same as the one I'd seen several times this week. I tilted the stone so Trace could see the serpent etched into the side of this stone. It felt almost intoxicating to cradle such power in my hands. I could see where it could easily overpower those who held it. Without the stasis spell, I would have fallen under its spell as well.

But El Serpiente, as Miss Elva had explained, wasn't evil. It pulsed with love – pure unadulterated love and kindness. I just wanted to curl up with it and hold it. Tears of pure joy were beginning to leak from my eyes and I caught myself squealing into my regulator. It was, I imagined, like stepping into the presence of an angel.

Closing my eyes and taking a deep breath, I tucked the stone into the side pouch of my BCD, opposite the bulge of the item Miss Elva had given me. Motioning to Trace, who had a similar giddy look around his eyes, we left the hull. Squeezing through the hole in the deck, we began our ascent, clicking our lights off and locking arms by habit.

I found myself giggling as we kicked around at our three-minute safety stop, happiness coursing through me from the stone tucked at my waist. A part of me wondered why anyone would let this stone go.

Or was that its draw? Pure happiness – would that eventually make you go mad? Is that why it had a sister stone – to temper the pure joy? Were they perfect as a whole and deadly, each in their own way, apart?

My mind clouded by joy, I ripped my regulator out almost before we hit the surface of the water.

"Trace!" I gasped, laughing as I flung my arms around his neck at the surface. "We did it!"

"That's good to hear, Hermosa. We've been waiting for you."

Chapter Thirty-Six

I WHIPPED MY head around as lights flashed on us from all angles. We were surrounded by three boats, and there were several people on Trace's boat as well. All with flashlights.

And all with guns trained on us.

"Trace, no," I gasped, grabbing hold of the ladder. Trace wrapped an arm around me and squeezed the button on my BCD hose, inflating my vest.

"Hermosa, you've been sneaky these last few nights. Good thing we've been able to track your boat. It's so easy to plant a tracking device when there's no security on the docks all night."

Trace cursed next to me and I shook my head at him. "It's not your fault."

Adrenaline coursed through me; it was the strangest sensation – I couldn't stop myself from smiling because of the godstone, yet I was simultaneously terrified for my life.

"We'll take the stone, Hermosa. Or stones? I'm not sure what you've picked up down there, but I'm assuming it's at least one of them." Tlaloc smiled at me all friendly-like, and I grinned back at him like a maniacal cheerleader.

"Don't give it to him, Althea. You can't," Trace hissed.

"Shut up or I'll shut you up," said a man on Trace's boat, kneeling so the barrel of the gun was inches from Trace's face.

"It's fine, you can have it. It's not worth our lives, Trace," I said, reaching into my BCD and pulling out the stone. I held it above me in the water and handed it off to the man on the boat. He took it and immediately turned and handed it to Tlaloc, clearly reluctant to hold it for too long.

Tlaloc's face lit up with pleasure as the stone was passed to him, and he held it up in the light.

"This. This stone. El Serpiente has come home to its people!" Tlaloc kissed the stone and held it in the air amidst the cheers of his men surrounding us.

Tlaloc looked down at us, a smile still playing across his face.

"Thank you, Hermosa, you've been a tremendous help. I'm sorry I won't be needing your services any longer."

I cringed and instinctively ducked my face under the water. I don't know why; not like I'd be able to dodge the bullets from twenty different guns. But when nothing happened, I poked my face back up, sputtering in the waves.

"Let go of the ladder."

It dawned on me suddenly what he meant to do. It was stunning in its simplicity, a beautiful plan. It was clear why Tlaloc made such a fierce leader.

"No, please, don't do this. I gave you the stone. Spare us," I begged.

"No loose ends, Hermosa. *Vaya con dios*," Tlaloc said, saluting me with the stone.

"Let go of the ladder or I will shoot you in the face," said the man on Trace's boat, and we both let go, hooking our arms together tightly.

"My boat," Trace whimpered. I didn't blame him. It was his everything.

"They're going to abandon it somewhere and let it drift. If they find our bodies it'll just look like a diving accident gone wrong," I said bitterly.

Trace swore, long and loudly, as he wrapped his arms around me.

"Hook your legs around my waist," he said, pulling me tight against his body. I wrapped my legs around his waist and hooked my arms around his neck, pushing my face close to his. It was a somewhat awkward way to hold each other in the water, but with our BCDs inflated, we were able to keep our faces above water.

I closed my eyes as the engines fired up and the boats took off, not able to bear watching Trace's boat drive away. Well, any of the boats, really.

Because now we were floating at sea, at night, without any way to get help.

If the sharks didn't get us, the ocean would.

Chapter Thirty-Seven

I ONLY FREAKED out for like a minute or two, tops. But once I'd gone through a few hysterical moments, I calmed down. Mostly.

"Shh, Thea, it's going to be okay. People know where we are. If we don't text after the dive they'll come looking for us."

"Yeah, but did you notice how quickly we're moving, here? We've caught a current," I moaned, as the mainland faded further away from sight.

"Just breathe. We're okay for the moment," Trace said against my neck, just as a wave smashed us in the face.

I spluttered out the water. "Wind's picking up," I commented.

"If need be, we'll put our regs in. We've got air still," Trace pointed out.

"Okay, okay, okay, calm down, Althea," I lectured myself.

Not going to lie – it wasn't easy. Being at sea in the pitch-black night with waves kicking up and no way to be found was not my idea of a fun night.

To be found.

To find and be found.

"Trace!" I squealed, tightening my legs around his waist.

"Althea, as much as I would like to get romantic with you, now is probably not the time," Trace joked, and I realized that I was rubbing up on… well, certain parts of his anatomy.

"Um, sorry. I just remembered something my mother told me," I said.

"Well, mentioning your mother is one way to rid me of my lusty thoughts," Trace observed dryly.

"The finding spell. My mom called me from halfway across the world and insisted I learn the finding spell. I thought at the time it had to do with finding the treasure. But it can be used inversely – to be found."

I almost squealed in his ear again, and he hugged me tighter to him as we drifted in the water.

"So now might be a good time to do that," Trace pointed out.

"Oh, right – okay, let me remember it."

I thought back to the spell, then prayed I had the words right.

"By the moon, sun, earth, air, fire, and sea,

Where we are now lost, draw help to me."

I focused on calling upon the elements, and being sure to follow up the spell with my intent.

"I intend for Luna and Miss Elva to find us."

"Good, I hope they do," Trace said into my ear.

"Shh," I said. Closing my eyes, I repeated the spell three times – and on the third, I felt the pulse of magick begin to surround me.

"I feel something!" Trace exclaimed.

"It's working," I said. "Now we wait."

The push of magick continued to throb around us, its beat insistent, cocooning us in its spell. It wasn't long before I heard something.

"Here!" I screeched, making Trace jump.

"Dang, Althea, that was my ear."

"I swear I heard someone calling."

"Althea!"

"Rafe!" I shouted back, surprised and yet not. There was no way anyone else could have reached us so quickly. "Rafe, here we are!" I lifted my flashlight and waved it back and forth.

"There you two are! Miss Elva told me to come find you. There are boats on the way. A police boat and everything!"

"How did the police know about us?" I asked, genuinely confused.

"Miss Elva got a feeling and alerted the Coast Guard. Turns out they were already on their way out, tracking some other boats."

"There! I see lights!" I pointed to the horizon where I could just make out the flashing lights of a police boat.

"I've got to go tell my lovemountain. Keep shining your flashlights so she can point the boats your way."

And with that Rafe zipped away.

Trace and I waved our flashlights frantically, and I looked up at the sky, silently thanking the goddesses for looking out for us.

"Trace, I have to tell you something."

"You dream about me naked?"

"Haha. I gave Tlaloc a fake stone."

"What! How?"

"Miss Elva gave me a dummy stone. Said she felt like I would need it. I have the real one on me."

"Is that why I feel so damn happy, even though I'm trying not to panic about sharks?"

"Yup. It's in my BCD, along with the cross I took for Rafe."

"So the good guys win?"

"So long as we don't get eaten by a shark in the next five minutes? Yeah, I think we're good."

It was more like one minute; Rafe must have gotten to Miss Elva quickly. In moments a boat was drawing close, a searchlight hanging from the front. I shielded my eyes as it blinded us.

"Sorry about that," a voice said as they cut the engines and threw us a life ring. I closed my eyes as I hooked an arm around the ring, then looked up at the owner of the voice.

"Hey, Nicola. Fancy seeing you here."

Chapter Thirty-Eight

It was only after we'd rescued Trace's boat, watched an enraged Tlaloc being loaded into a paddy wagon, and were wrapped in towels back at the dock that we finally got to talk to Luna and Miss Elva.

"So she's one of the good guys?" Trace asked, as we watched Nicola cross her arms and nod as a police officer lead another handcuffed man down the dock.

"Looks like it."

Nicola spoke with the officer briefly and then detoured to where the four of us sat.

"I'm sorry I couldn't tell you," Nicola said immediately, her British accent long gone.

"I can't believe I didn't read it on you," I admitted, a little embarrassed that my psychic powers had failed me.

"I studied up on how to block you from reading my mind. I'm sorry – I work for a private firm that investigate stolen art cases. They've honed in on El Serpiente and we were trying our best to recover it. We get a little more intensive training when we're on a case like this."

"Is that why you stayed on the boat? To make sure nobody hijacked us?"

"Yes. That's also why I specifically ordered you to stop diving once I confirmed – or thought I had confirmed – where the treasure was. I didn't need you two getting hurt." Nicola sighed and shook her head at us. "And yet, it was still a close call. Luckily we'd been tracking Tlaloc pretty closely – worried that he would interfere when we were finally so close. When he actually stepped onto a boat tonight, we knew he had to have found the treasure. That emerald is amazing, isn't it?"

"Just stunning. What are your plans for it?" I asked, lying through my teeth.

"I think once all the paperwork is done, it will go to a private gallery. El Serpiente is a famous historical piece. It deserves to be on display – and it will command a high price."

"How come some art firm is involved in this anyway?" I asked.

"I can't share that with you. Other than we've been following Tlaloc and his plans for a while – he's crossed international borders illegally and has run some pretty major operations. This isn't the first piece of treasure that he's gone after."

I nodded at Nicola.

Miss Elva didn't say a word. And as far as I was concerned, Miss Elva trumped some private art detective agency or whatever Nicola was. She obviously had her own plans for the stones, and I trusted her implicitly.

I wondered if we'd have to return the money we had been paid.

"Nicola, what about the money in our accounts?"

Nicola waved her hand.

"Keep it. You won't be getting the rest of it, but you can keep what's already been transferred. Too much paperwork to transfer it back. It's a business expense."

My eyes grew wide – that was some business expense. The art world must pay well.

A crowd had begun to gather at the dock – with all the police activity, I'm sure people thought someone had drowned. I gasped in surprise as Cash pushed his way through the crowd and stormed over to where we sat.

I stood up – a bit shaky on my feet, and a bit shaky as to where we stood as a couple.

Cash stopped in front of me, visibly agitated as he surveyed me.

"You're okay."

"I am. I'm safe."

"Do I even want to know?"

I shook my head, feeling my heart cracking open a bit.

Cash reached out and pulled me in for a quick tight hug, and I blinked back the tears that threatened. Stepping back, he kept his hands on my shoulders.

"I'm going back to Miami for a while. I'm not sure how long. I don't know where we stand – I'd hoped I wouldn't keep finding you in these situations. I don't know how I feel. I… I can't stop thinking about you. And yet I can't live with you constantly putting yourself in the line of danger."

"I know," I whispered, fighting for control as I looked up at him. "Maybe we are just too different."

"Maybe we are. But you know, I honestly thought we'd beat the odds." Cash shrugged and looked away for a moment before looking back at me. Reaching up, he ran a finger down my cheek. "Take care of yourself."

I blinked back tears as I watched him walk away – completely unsure if I was letting one of the best things that had ever happened to me just walk out of my life.

"That guy," Trace shook his head in disgust.

Miss Elva chuckled.

"Honey, there's plenty of fish in the sea. Don't you be forgetting that."

Epilogue

LATER THAT NIGHT we all stood in Miss Elva's living room as she held both stones in her hands.

"Four hundred years they've been separated. Maybe all they wanted to do was be back together."

The stones – bigger than Miss Elva's hands – began to glow and pulse, as if sensing each other's nearness.

I missed holding El Serpiente. It had been like mainlining joy. But too much happiness wasn't good for people. You can't know joy without knowing pain.

And even though I was in a lot of pain right now, it was important for me to feel it. Because if I didn't feel it, how would I learn from it?

See? I'm maturing.

"Wow," I breathed, watching as Miss Elva slid the stones together along the grooves that joined them. We jumped as they emitted a brilliant flash of light and one crystal clear *ding!* The etchings of the rose and the serpent glowed a brilliant green before the stone quieted down – content to be together again as one.

Miss Elva lowered the complete stone into a gilded box and pulled the cover tight, locking it with a key.

"Where will this go?"

"I have a friend who'll return it to its rightful place – at a temple high in the mountains of Mexico that still survives and operates to this day."

"But what if it falls into the wrong hands again?"

"It's meant to be with its people – the legend lives on through them. We can no more contain it and put it on display than we can decide where it belongs. The godstones know where they're meant to be."

"Oh! Rafe, I have something for you," I exclaimed, having forgotten in all the craziness. I went over to the couch, where my bag was tucked next to Hank.

"A gift!" Rafe exclaimed. "For me?"

Reaching into the bag, I pulled out the intricate cross I had tucked in my BCD earlier in the night. It was no longer than the length of my hand, and the workmanship was exquisite. Turning, I held it out to him.

"I know you can't hold this. But I thought you'd like to at least have it in the house with you. A souvenir of your pirating days."

Rafe floated over to me and hovered above my hand, looking in awe from my face back to my palm. His eyes grew huge in his face, and I was astonished to see a sheen of tears film his eyes.

"My mother's cross. You brought my mother's cross home to me. It was the only thing I had of hers."

"I didn't know. I just saw it and knew it was for you. I'm glad I could bring it back to you," I said, realizing I wasn't going to be able to hold back my tears either.

"My mother's cross. Oh – oh, she loved me so. And I her," Rafe turned, embarrassed as he wiped his tears. He flitted over to Miss Elva. "Do you see, lovemountain? Do you see the beautiful cross my mother gave me? She would have loved you."

Miss Elva's eyes grew wide as saucers at that comment.

"Now you know I'm not about meeting no parents, Rafe. I don't do in-laws." She hooted out her huge laugh and lifted the cross from my hand. Holding it to the light, she nodded.

"But this? This is a good piece. We'll put it in a place of honor, and you'll tell me all about her," Miss Elva said, walking away with Rafe babbling after her. He shot me a look over his shoulder.

"Thank you, psychic."

"No problem, pirate. Be nice to my dog from now on."

Miss Elva's chuckle followed me as I picked up my bag and left the house.

Trace and Luna followed me out.

We all looked at each other in question.

"See you at Lucky's?" Luna asked.

"Oh yeah, Beau's going to lose his shit when he hears about this."

I laughed as we headed for Trace's Jeep, Hank at my side. Maybe there was a small hole in my heart from Cash, but I always had my friends to fill it.

And maybe that's what El Serpiente had wanted to tell me about love.

Read an Excerpt from Tequila Knots & Valentine Shots
An Althea Rose Valentine's Story

"That should be enough to add a little zing back into the bedroom," Miss Elva chuckled as she spilled a dash of oyster powder into a brilliant red liquid she was stirring in a copper bowl in her pint-sized kitchen. Howlin' Wolf poured out his pain on the CD player behind her and she sang along as she stirred, pitching her deep alto voice to match his gravelly one.

As the liquid began to turn crimson with purple undertones, Miss Elva stopped singing and focused on infusing the potion in front of her with the touch of magick she carried – *old* magick – the kind many of the new sect of ladies dabbling at witchcraft these days didn't seem to understand.

"Hacks is all they are," Miss Elva grumbled as she finished up her spell and went back to humming along with

Howlin' Wolf as she considered how to package her love potion.

Love Potion No. 7, to be specific. Love Potion No. 9 was nothing to be trifled with.

Miss Elva bumped her considerable girth around the kitchen, shaking her hips as she sang along to the music, her mind on the couple she was concocting the potion for. Sheila had come to her because her marriage had ground to a halt in the bedroom. Miss Elva had done a quick reading of her energy just to make sure that there wasn't anything else going on that was contributing to the absence of the bedroom boogie-woogie. All she'd found was a lot of love between the two that just needed a little kick to get moving again. And Love Potion No. 7 was the perfect antidote to their problem.

Tonight would be a perfect night for it too – being Valentine's Day and all. Miss Elva was already considering what outfit she would be wearing to the Lonely Hearts Valentine's Day party at Lucky's Tiki Bar later that evening. She'd need to make a statement, of course.

"What are you doing?" a voice demanded.

Miss Elva continued to concentrate on stirring the liquid as she spoke over her shoulder.

"Making a love potion," she said to Rafe, who was hovering just behind her.

Rafe, her pirate ghost, had been acquired when her friend Althea had botched learning how to cast a circle. He'd slipped easily through the veil and although Althea and her white witch best friend, Luna, had tried to get rid of him, it had only taken one look between Rafe and Miss Elva to seal his fate.

Some might call it love at first sight.

To sign up for notification of new releases, please go HERE.

Please consider leaving a review! A book can live or die by the reviews alone. It means a lot to an author to receive reviews, and I greatly appreciate it!

Other books by Tricia O'Malley

THE MYSTIC COVE SERIES
Wild Irish Roots
Wild Irish Heart
Wild Irish Eyes
Wild Irish Soul
Wild Irish Rebel
Wild Irish Roots: Margaret & Sean
Wild Irish Witch

THE ALTHEA ROSE SERIES
One Tequila
Tequila for Two
Tequila Will Kill Ya
Three Tequilas
Tequila Shots & Valentine Knots

THE STOLEN DOG
A non-fiction account of our dog being stolen and how we recovered him. All proceeds go to animal rescues.

Author's Note

Thank you for taking a chance on my books; it means the world to me. Writing novels came by way of a tragedy that turned into something beautiful and larger than itself (see: The Stolen Dog). Since that time, I've changed my career, put it all on the line, and followed my heart. Thank you for taking part in the worlds I have created; I hope you enjoy it.

I would be honored if you left a review online. It helps other readers to take a chance on my work.

As always, you can reach me at omalley.tricia@gmail.com or feel free to visit my website at triciaomalley.com.

You can sign up for new releases here
http://eepurl.com/1LAiz.

Author's Acknowledgement

First and foremost, I would like to thank my husband for his unending support as I pursue this wildly creative career of being an author. It isn't easy to watch someone follow the creative path, and uncertainties are rampant. Josh, thanks for being my rock.

I'd like to thank my family and friends for their constant support and all of my beta readers for their excellent feedback.

Thank you to Elayne Morgan for a fantastic job at editing!

And last, but never least, my two constant companions as I struggle through words on my computer each day - Briggs and Blue.